AIDING AND ABETTING

MURIEL SPARK DBE, CLit, FRSE, FRSL was born in Edinburgh in 1918. A poet, essayist, biographer and novelist, she won much international praise, receiving the James Tait Black Memorial Prize in 1965 for *The Mandelbaum Gate*, the US Ingersoll Foundation TS Eliot Award in 1992 and the David Cohen Prize in 1997. She was twice shortlisted for the Booker Prize (for *The Public Image* in 1969 and *Loitering with Intent* in 1981) and, in 2010, was shortlisted for the 'Lost Man Booker Prize' of 1970. In 1993 Muriel Spark was made a Dame for services to literature. In 1998 she was awarded the Golden PEN Award for a 'Lifetime's Distinguished Service to Literature'. She died in Tuscany in 2006.

LOUISE WELSH studied history at the University of Glasgow after which she ran a second-hand bookshop. Her first novel, *The Cutting Room* (1992), won the Crime Writers' Association Creasey Dagger for the best first crime novel. Its successor, *Tamburlaine Must Die*, fictionalised the last days of the Elizabethan playwright Christopher Marlowe. Other novels include *The Bullet Trick* (2006), *Naming the Bones* (2010) and *The Girl on the Stairs* (2012). *A Lovely Way to Burn*, published in 2014, was the first part of the 'Plague Times' trilogy, of which *Death Is a Welcome Guest* and *No Dominion* are the two concluding volumes. She is currently Professor of Creative Literature at the University of Glasgow.

Novels by Muriel Spark in Polygon

The Comforters
Robinson
Memento Mori
The Ballad of Peckham Rye
The Bachelors
The Prime of Miss Jean Brodie
The Girls of Slender Means
The Mandelbaum Gate
The Public Image
The Driver's Seat
Not to Disturb
The Hothouse by the East River
The Abbess of Crewe
The Takeover
Territorial Rights
Loitering with Intent
The Only Problem
A Far Cry from Kensington
Symposium
Reality and Dreams
Aiding and Abetting
The Finishing School

AIDING
AND ABETTING

Muriel Spark

Introduced by Louise Welsh

This edition published in Great Britain in 2018
by Polygon, an imprint of Birlinn Ltd.

Birlinn Ltd
West Newington House
10 Newington Road
Edinburgh
EH9 1QS

www.polygonbooks.co.uk

1

ISBN 978 1 84697 445 8

The publisher gratefully acknowledges investment from
Creative Scotland towards the publication of this book.

Supported by the Muriel Spark Society

British Library Cataloguing-in-Publication Data
A catalogue record for this book is available
on request from the British Library.

Typeset by Biblichor Ltd, Edinburgh
Printed and bound in Malta by Gutenberg Press

Foreword

Muriel Spark was born in Edinburgh on the first of February, 1918. She was the second child of Cissy and Bernard Camberg, an engineer from a family of Jewish and Lithuanian extraction. Her early life is recalled in loving and meticulous detail in her autobiography, *Curriculum Vitae*, published in 1992. Hers was a working-class upbringing, but while money was tight she was in no way deprived. Her mother was gregarious and extrovert, always singing songs and telling stories, and wearing the kind of clothes that made her unmissable among other, more dully dressed women in the Bruntsfield neighbourhood.

When she was five years old Spark began her education at James Gillespie's High School for Girls where she remained until she was sixteen. It was a period she remembered with great fondness. She was anointed the school's 'Poet and Dreamer' and many of her early verses appeared in its magazine. In 1929, she first encountered an inspirational teacher, a spinster called Christina Kay, who was to have a formative effect on her life. It was Miss Kay, for example, who took her and her friends – 'the crème de la crème' – on long walks through the city's Old Town, to exhibitions, concerts and poetry readings, and who insisted that she must become a writer. 'I felt I had hardly much choice in the matter,' Spark wrote later. In her sixth and most famous novel, *The Prime of Miss Jean Brodie*, the main character was modelled closely, if not actually, on Miss Kay. Like the unorthodox Miss Brodie, Miss Kay was an Italophile and a naive admirer of Mussolini, of whom she pinned a picture on a wall together with paintings by Renaissance masters.

On leaving school Spark enrolled in a course for précis-writing at Heriot-Watt College. She then found a job as secretary to the owner of a department store in Princes Street, the Scottish capital's main thoroughfare. At a dance she met Sydney Oswald Spark, a lapsed Jew, whose initials she felt in hindsight should have warned her to steer clear of him. Like her father's parents, 'SOS' had been born in Lithuania. She was nineteen, he was thirty-two. He planned to teach in Africa, and Muriel, eager to leave Edinburgh and launch herself at life, agreed to become engaged. In August 1937, she followed him to Southern Rhodesia (now Zimbabwe) and the following month they were married. Their son, Robin, was born in 1938. Soon thereafter the couple separated.

The outbreak of war the following year meant Spark could not return home as she had hoped and she had no option but to stay in Africa. In 1944, however, she obtained a divorce and returned to Britain on a troop ship. Having settled her son with her parents, she headed for London where the devastation of the Blitz was everywhere evident. She boarded at the Helena Club, the original of the May of Teck Club in *The Girls of Slender Means*, and found work in the Political Intelligence department of the Foreign Office, whose *raison d'être* was to disseminate anti-Nazi propaganda among the German population.

In the years immediately after the war she attempted to make a living as a writer. In 1947, she was appointed General Secretary of the Poetry Society and editor of its magazine, *Poetry Review*, but she fell foul of traditionalists, including Marie Stopes, a pioneer of birth control. It was a pity, Spark remarked, 'that her mother rather than she had not thought of birth control'. Her first book, *A Tribute to Wordsworth*, was co-written with her then lover, Derek Stanford, and published in 1950. A year later she won a short story competition in the *Observer* newspaper with 'The Seraph and the Zambesi'. In 1952, she published her debut collection of poetry, *The Fanfarlo and Other Verse*.

Her conversion to Catholicism in 1954 coincided with her beginning work on her first novel, *The Comforters*, which finally appeared in 1957. Praised by Graham Greene and Evelyn Waugh among others, it allowed Spark to give up part-time secretarial work and devote herself to writing. Four more novels – *Robinson*, *Memento Mori*, *The Ballad of Peckham Rye* and *The Bachelors*, and a collection of stories, *The Go-Away Bird* – followed in quick succession and enhanced her reputation for originality and wit.

It was with the publication in 1961 of *The Prime of Miss Jean Brodie*, however, that Spark became an international bestseller. It was turned into a play and a film for which Maggie Smith, who played the eponymous teacher, won the Oscar for Best Actress. Indeed, remarked Spark, so closely did Smith become associated with the part that many readers seemed to assume that she was her creator. The novel, which Spark liked to refer to as her 'milch cow', was a critical as well as a commercial success and continued to sell well throughout its author's long career. In America, it was first published in *The New Yorker*. Its editor, William Shawn, gave Spark an office in which to work. There, she wrote her next two novels, *The Girls of Slender Means* and *The Mandelbaum Gate*, which was awarded the James Tait Black Memorial Prize.

In 1967, having grown tired of the clamour and claustrophobia of life in New York, she moved to Italy and Rome.

That same year she was made an OBE. It also saw the publication of her first collected volumes of stories and poems. Novels continued to appear at regular intervals. *The Public Image* appeared in 1968 and was shortlisted for the Booker Prize. *The Driver's Seat*, which Spark believed to be her best, was published in 1970. In 1974 came *The Abbess of Crewe*, an inspired satire of the Watergate scandal, which she set in a convent.

In the mid 1970s Spark left Rome for Tuscany, settling in a rambling and venerable house deep in the countryside, owned by her friend, Penelope Jardine, an artist. Surrounded by fields of vines and olives, she was able to work without fear of interruption. *The Takeover*, *Territorial Rights* and *Loitering with Intent* – also shortlisted for the Booker – were among the first novels she wrote in the place that would be her final home. Among the many awards she received were the Ingersoll Foundation TS Eliot Award, the Scottish Arts Council Award for *Reality and Dreams*, the Boccaccio Prize for European Literature, the David Cohen British Literature Prize for a lifetime's achievement, and the Golden PEN Award from PEN International. In 1993, she was made a Dame.

Though in her later years she was often beset by illness, she never stopped writing. It was her calling and she pursued it with unfailing dedication. She always had a poem 'on the go' and she never wanted for ideas for novels and stories and plays. Among her later novels were *A Far Cry from Kensington*, *Symposium*, *Reality and Dreams* and *Aiding and Abetting*. Her valedictory novel was *The Finishing School*, the majority of whose characters are would-be writers, which was published in 2004. Spark died two years later at the age of eighty-eight and is buried in the walled cemetery of the village of Oliveto in the Val di Chiana. On her headstone, she is described in Italian with one simple word: *poeta*.

Introduction

Louise Welsh

> The seventh Earl has been missing since the night of 7th
> November 1974 when his wife was taken to hospital, severely
> wounded in her head, and the body of his children's nanny
> was found battered, in a mail sack, in his house.

Muriel Spark's opening note to readers outlines the essential known facts about the disappearance of Lord Lucan.
Spark reminds us that the novel is a work of fiction and
continues:

> What we know about 'Lucky' Lucan, his words, his habits,
> his attitude to people and to life, from his friends, photo-
> graphs and police records, I have absorbed creatively, and
> metamorphosed into what I have written.

The implication is that fiction contains truths that lie beyond
mere factual accounts of dates, events and actions. Spark
adds almost as an afterthought, 'The parallel story of a fake
stigmatic is also based on fact.'

The fake stigmatic is Dr Hildegard Wolf aka Beate
Pappenheim who has abandoned a lucrative life as a living
saint. She is now a psychiatrist with a successful, though
unorthodox, practice in Paris, where she is treating not

one, but two Lord Lucans. Both Lords may be imposters. Whether they are acting alone or in tandem is initially unclear.

Aiding and Abetting, Spark's twenty-first novel, was published in 2000 when she was eighty-two. Lucky Lucan, once a staple of tabloid exposés, broadsheet supplements and the punchline of variety show jokes was slipping from public consciousness, the murder and its surrounding mystery barely known of by a generation, 'who were too young or even unborn at the time'.

In notes for the novel, lodged in the National Library of Scotland's Muriel Spark Archive, Spark writes, 'the study of Lucan is the study of evil'. The title of the book, *Aiding and Abetting*, suggests the evil is not confined to the Earl, but is shared by loyal friends and associates – aiders and abetters – who sheltered him in the hours after the murder of his children's nanny, Sandra Rivett. The jury at the inquest into Rivett's death declared the cause to be 'murder by Lord Lucan'. A warrant committing Lucan for trial was issued immediately after the verdict, but his disappearance meant no hearing could take place. The question of whether he committed suicide or escaped abroad became a national obsession.

There were rumours the Earl had shot himself, was eaten by tigers in a private zoo, jumped from a ferry, was kidnapped by the IRA, descended into a bottomless pothole. Shortly after his disappearance, the *Guardian* reported that witnesses had seen him 'driving drunk up the M1, buying flowers on a London street and getting on a train in Edinburgh'. Gossip (strongly rejected by Hill's family) had Lucan fleeing the country in a private jet flown by racing driver Graham Hill. In 1994 *The Times* reported that police officers continued to follow up fifty to sixty sightings of the Earl a year. He had been spotted 'working as a waiter in San Francisco, at an alcoholics' centre in Brisbane, at a hotel in Madagascar, in Botswana, Hong Kong and the Orkneys'. The satirical television show *Spitting Image* regularly featured a Lord Lucan puppet who appeared in the background of sketches, dressed as a waiter and serving drinks.

Press attention consistently focused on the 'playboy Earl' and his set – lion tamers, racing drivers, nightclub owners, gamblers and aristocrats. Little attention was spared for Sandra Rivett, a young, working-class Irish woman brutally battered to death.

Aiding and Abetting treads a fine line between humour and repulsion. If Lucan did indeed escape, it was with the help of aiders and abetters who placed the freedom of the Earl above justice for Sandra Rivett and who treated the fact that he mistakenly murdered his children's nanny, rather than his wife, as a 'bungle'.

Spark wrote in her notes for *Aiding and Abetting* that 'the theme of the novel is blood'. The bloody murder at the centre of the Lucan mystery reappears and repeats throughout the text, a true crime story underpinning the satire.

Sandra was bashed and bludgeoned. She was stuffed into a sack. Bashed also was Lucan's wife when she came down to see what was the matter. She was bashed and bloodied . . . 'Nanny Rivett was killed in error.' 'And the hack-and-bash job on Lady Lucan?' 'That was different. She should have died.' . . . Blood on his hands. Blood all over his clothes . . . it was horrible bloody slaughter . . . His wife covered with blood . . . blood all over his trousers . . . blood oozing from the mailbag . . . the girl with all that blood . . . he had meant those thuds for his wife . . . mess and blood . . .

The theme of blood extends to Beate/Hildegard. When Beate Pappenheim was an impoverished medical student studying in Munich in the 1970s, she used her menstrual blood to simulate stigmata in order to extort money from credulous believers. When her con was discovered Beate fled overseas, became Hildegard Wolf and established a successful practice and happy home life. She would have sworn that the Beate Pappenheim of her past was a 'different person' from herself . . . She had just put Beate out of her mind, destroying her old birth certificate and replacing it with a new one obtained from a lawyer in Marseilles.

But Hildegard discovers it is not easy to escape past misdemeanours. The two Lord Lucans have learned of her criminal history and intend to blackmail her. Spark writes in her notes: 'Hildegard's crime is small compared to Lucan's but they are both on the run.'

Aiding and Abetting delights in doubles. The two Lucans are doppelgängers of sorts, physically alike, their fates bound together. Spark was born and educated in Edinburgh, the city that helped birth James Hogg's *The Private Memoirs and Confessions of a Justified Sinner* and Robert Louis Stevenson's *Strange Case of Dr Jekyll and Mr Hyde*. Both novels feature diabolical twinned protagonists. The two Lord Lucans have grown to hate each other, but their existences are so intertwined that, in the tradition of doppelgängers, for one to spill the other's blood may be to invite his own death.

Blood also features in terms of social status. Lucan and his set consider themselves superior to Rivett's class by virtue of their blue blood. 'There must be something about the lower orders they bleed so,' muses one of the Lucans at a dinner with Hildegard, where he absorbs red wine 'like blotting paper'. The supposed thinness of working-class blood is returned to more than once. 'Perhaps murdered nannies have more blood to spill than the upper class,' suggests Benny Rolfe, one of Lucan's fictional sponsors.

Benny describes the murder as 'a bungle like any other bungle', adding that if the Earl had succeeded in killing his wife that 'would not have been a bungle'.

'Hadn't anyone any feelings for the poor lovely nurse-girl?' asks Lacey, daughter of Maria Twickenham whose estranged husband is another Lucan aider and abetter. A descendant of the Lucan set, Lacey considers herself beyond the snobbery of her parents' generation, but manages to patronise Sandra Rivett with a surfeit of adjectives and no courtesy of a name. She would like to write a book about Lucan and pursues the Earl accompanied by his one-time friend Joe Murray. Murray has his own theory about why Lucan's associates protected him: 'psychological paralysis'. He compares Lucan's disappearance to the escape of Burgess and Maclean. 'They got away purely on the hypnosis of their life-stylish act.'

'We could have had Lucky asleep in one of our spare rooms and they [the police] would never have found out,' declared one of the actual Lucan set in correspondence with Spark. The letter-writer described the police as 'dear boys' but out of their depth. Another friend of Lucan, who waited four days before informing police he had visited her house after the crime, stated, 'It's the police's problem, actually. They're obviously trained to discern these things.' For their part the police christened Lucan's friends 'the Eton Mafia' and accused the aristocracy of closing ranks.

It was not only his immediate circle who refused to reject Lord Lucan. He lived on vicariously in the British aristocracy. Lucan's entry in *Who's Who* continued to be listed, the final line, where his current address should be recorded, kept tactfully blank. His coat peg in the House of Lords remained untouched, as if waiting for the Earl's return. Lucan's son and heir's initial efforts to claim the title, more than twenty years after his disappearance, were rejected on the grounds of 'insufficient evidence' that the Earl was deceased.

By the time readers encounter Lucan in *Aiding and Abetting* the seventh Earl is in his mid-sixties and has recently been declared dead. He tells Hildegard that he has come to think of himself 'as a dead man. It distresses me.' His aiders and abetters are 'sick, dead, changed or changing'.

Maria Twickenham cannot understand why she went along with her husband's concealment of Lord Lucan.

> the memory was like that pill-box veiled hat she had found among her old things, dating from the early 'seventies, last worn at the Derby. She could not wear that hat any more, nor could she again accept her husband's concealment of Lucan.

More than a quarter of a century has passed since the murder and Maria has changed. 'Habits change. States of mind change. Collective moods change.' Hildegard is also transformed. She has left Beate Pappenheim behind. It seems only Lord Lucan is incapable of reinventing himself.

It is worth remembering that Spark attended the Eichmann trial, an experience that sat at the heart of her 1965 novel *The Mandelbaum Gate*. Eichmann, a leading Nazi who escaped capture after World War Two, was eventually brought to trial in 1961. He was found guilty of crimes against humanity and sentenced to death, but refused to accept his guilt.

It would be crass to directly compare Lucan and Eichmann, but 'the banality of evil' and the impossibility of escaping moral responsibility for murder, no matter what systems or elites one belongs to, are at the centre of *Aiding and Abetting*. Lucan evaded trial with the help of fellow members of a wealthy elite. But *Aiding and Abetting* does not allow him to get away with the murder of Sandra Rivett. The Earl has acquired a double, a mirror image who roots him in what he is. His crime is too big, too evil, to be dismissed. Murder rather than his rank or disappearance is what defines him.

Publication of *Aiding and Abetting* prompted a variety of reactions. Lady Lucan described the book as 'absurd and insensitive' and showing 'a lack of feeling for people who are still living with the events.' An inmate of HMP Long Lartin wrote to Spark claiming to be 'one of those Lucky Lucan rang on the fatal night'. He outlined his version of events and told her that 'her inventions are hopelessly misconceived'. Another unsolicited correspondent detailed a meeting in a travel agency with a man she was sure was Lord Lucan. A letter from the wife of a former friend of Lucan suggested the Earl had been murdered by hitmen and asked Spark if she had any knowledge of a lesbian angle in the case.

The correspondents missed the point. Spark never intended to establish the events of the night of 7th November 1974 or Lucan's subsequent disappearance. She merely shows us what he is and in so doing holds him and his aiders and abetters to account. In a blood-stained letter to a friend written on the night of Sandra Rivett's murder, Lord Lucan declared his intention to 'lie doggo for a bit'. Muriel Spark drags him to the page, 'suave, casually dressed, rich, manicured, simply awful'.

NOTE TO READERS

The following story, like all those connected with the seventh Earl of Lucan, is based on hypothesis.

The seventh Earl has been missing since the night of 7th November 1974 when his wife was taken to hospital, severely wounded in her head, and the body of his children's nanny was found battered, in a mailsack, in his house. He left two ambiguous letters.

Since then he has been wanted on charges of murder and attempted murder, of which he was found guilty by a coroner's jury. He has not shown up to face trial in the criminal courts.

The seventh Earl was officially declared dead in 1999, his body has never been found, although he has been 'sighted' in numerous parts of the world, predominantly central Africa. The story of his presumed years of clandestine wanderings, his nightmare existence since his disappearance, remains a mystery, and I have no doubt would differ factually and in actual feeling from the story I have told. What we know about 'Lucky' Lucan, his words, his habits, his attitudes to people and to life, from his friends, photographs and police records, I have absorbed creatively, and metamorphosed into what I have written.

The parallel 'story' of a fake stigmatic woman is also based on fact.

M. S.

I

The receptionist looked tinier than ever as she showed the tall, tall, Englishman into the studio of Dr Hildegard Wolf, the psychiatrist who had come from Bavaria, then Prague, Dresden, Avila, Marseilles, then London, and now settled in Paris.

'I have come to consult you,' he said, 'because I have no peace of mind. Twenty-five years ago I sold my soul to the Devil.' The Englishman spoke in a very foreign French.

'Would you feel easier,' she said, 'if we spoke in English? I am an English speaker of a sort since I was a student.'

'Far easier,' he said, 'although, in a sense, it makes the reality more distressing. What I have to tell you is an English story.'

Dr Wolf's therapeutic methods had been perfected by herself. They had made her virtually the most successful psychiatrist in Paris, or at least the most sought-after. At the same time she was tentatively copied; those who tried to do so generally failed. The method alone did not suffice. Her personality was needed as well.

What she did for the most part was talk about herself throughout the first three sessions, turning only casually on the problems of her patients; then, gradually, in an offhand way she would induce them to begin to discuss themselves. Some patients, angered, did not return after the first or at least second session, conducted on these lines.

Others remonstrated, 'Don't you want to hear about *my* problem?'

'No, quite frankly, I don't very much.'

Many, fascinated, returned to her studio and it was they who, so it was widely claimed, reaped their reward. By now her method was famous and even studied in the universities. The Wolf method.

'I sold my soul to the Devil.'

'Once in my life,' she said, 'I had a chance to do that. Only I wasn't offered enough. Let me tell you about it . . .'

He had heard that she would do just this. The friend who had recommended her to him, a priest who had been through her hands during a troubled period, told him, 'She advised me not to try to pray. She advised me to shut up and listen. Read the gospel, she said. Jesus is praying to you for sympathy. You have to see his point of view, what he had to put up with. Listen, don't talk. Read the Bible. Take it in. God is talking, not you.'

Her new patient sat still and listened, luxuriating in the expenditure of money which he would have found impossible only three weeks ago. For twenty-five years, since he was struck down in England by a disaster, he had been a furtive fugitive, always precariously beholden to his friends, his many friends, but still, playing the role of benefactors, their numbers diminishing. Three weeks ago his nickname Lucky had become a solidified fact. He was lucky. He had in fact discovered some money waiting for him on the death of one of his main aiders and abetters. It had been locked in a safe, waiting for him to turn up. He could afford to have a conscience. He could now consult at leisure one of the most expensive and most highly recommended psychiatrists in Paris. 'You have to listen to her, she makes you listen, first of all,' they said – 'they' being at least four people. He sat blissfully in his smart clothes and listened. He sat before her desk in a leather chair with arms; he lounged. It was strange how so many people of the past had been under the impression he had already collected the money left for him in a special account. Even his benefactor's wife had not known about its existence.

He might, in fact, have been anybody. But she arranged for the money to be handed over without a question. His name was Lucky and lucky he was indeed.

But money did not last. He gambled greatly.

The windows of Dr Wolf's consulting rooms on the Boulevard St Germain were double-glazed to allow only a pleasing hum of traffic to penetrate.

'I don't know how it struck you,' said Hildegard (Dr Wolf) to her patient. 'But to me, selling one's soul to the Devil involves murder. Anything less is not worthy of the designation. You can sell your soul to a number of agents, let's face it, but to the Devil there has to be a killing or so involved. In my case, it was many years ago, I was treating a patient who became psychologically dependent on me. A young man, not very nice. His problem was a tendency to suicide. One was tempted to encourage him in his desire. He was simply nasty, simply cruel. His fortune was immense. I was offered a sum of money by his cousin, the next of kin, to slide this awful young man down the slope. But I didn't. I sensed the meanness of the cousin, and doubted whether he would really have parted with the money once my patient was dead. I refused. Perhaps, if I had been offered a substantially larger sum, I would have made that pact with the Devil. Who knows? As it was, I said no, I wouldn't urge the awful young man to take his own life. In fact I encouraged him to live. But to do otherwise would have definitely, I think, led to his death and I would have been guilty of murder.'

'Did he ever take his life, then?'

'No, he is alive today.'

The Englishman was looking at Hildegard in a penetrating way as if to read her true thoughts. Perhaps he wondered if she was in fact trying to tell him that she doubted his story. He wanted to get away from her office, now. He had paid for his first session on demand, a very stiff fee, as he reckoned, of fifteen hundred dollars for three-quarters of an hour. But she talked on. He sat and listened with a large bulging leather brief-case at his feet.

For the rest of the period she told him she had been living in Paris now for over twelve years, and found it congenial to her way of life and her work. She told him she had a great many friends in the fields of medicine, music, religion and art, and although well into her forties, it was just possible she might still marry. 'But I would never give up my profession,' she said. 'I do so love it.'

His time was up, and she had not asked him a single question about himself. She took it for granted he would continue with her. She shook hands and told him to fix his next appointment with the receptionist. Which, in fact, he did.

It was towards the end of that month that Hildegard asked him her first question.

'What can I do for *you*?' she said, as if he was positively intruding on her professional time.

He gave her an arrogant look, sweeping her face. 'First,' he said, 'I have to tell you that I'm wanted by the police on two counts: murder and attempted murder. I have been wanted for over twenty years. I am the missing Lord Lucan.'

Hildegard was almost jolted at this. She was currently treating another patient who claimed, convincingly, to be the long-missing lord. She suspected collusion.

'I suppose,' said the man at present sitting in her office, 'that you know my story.' She did indeed know his story. She knew it as thoroughly as anyone could, except for the police, who naturally would keep some secrets to themselves.

Hildegard had gathered books, and obtained press-cuttings dating from 1974, when the scandal had broken, to the present day. It was a story that was forever cropping up. The man in front of her, aged about sixty-five, looked very like the latest police identikit of Lord Lucan, but so in a different way did the other patient.

The man sitting in front of her had reached down for his brief-case. 'The story is all here,' he said, tapping the bulging bag.

'Tell me about it,' she said.

Yes, in fact, let us all hear about it, once more. Those who were too young or even unborn at the time should be told, too. The Lord Lucan with whom this story is concerned was the seventh Earl of Lucan. He was born on 18th December 1934. He disappeared from the sight of his family and most of his friends on the night of 7th November 1974, under suspicion of having murdered his children's nanny and having attempted to murder his wife. The murder of the girl had been an awful mistake. He had thought, in the darkness of a basement, that she was his wife. The inquest into the death of the nanny, Sandra Rivett, ended in a verdict 'Murder by Lord Lucan' and a warrant for his arrest. As for his wife, Lady Lucan's account of the events of that night fitted in with the findings of the police in all relevant details. However, the police had one very strongly felt complaint: the missing Earl had been aided and abetted in his movements subsequent to the murder. His upper-class friends, said the police, had helped the suspect to get away and cover his tracks. They mocked the police, they stone-walled the enquiries. By the time Lord Lucan's trail had been followed to any likely destination he could have been far away, or dead by his own hand. Many, at the time, believed he had escaped to Africa, where he had friends and resources.

From time to time throughout the intervening years 'sightings' of the missing suspect have been reported. The legend has not been allowed to fade. On 9th July 1994 the *Daily Express* wrote about him and the frightful end of Sandra Rivett by mistaken identity.

> The work, it appeared, of a madman or someone deranged by pressure beyond his control . . . His cheques were bouncing all over smart Belgravia, the school fees had not been paid, he had overdrafted at four banks, borrowed money from a lender (at 18 per cent interest), £7,000 from playboy Taki and £3,000 from another Greek. His mentor, gambler Stephen Raphael, had also lent him £3,000.

On the night of 7th November 1974, the basement of his wife's house was dark. The light-bulb had been removed. Down the stairs came a woman. Lucan struck, not his wife but the nanny. 'When is Sandra's night off?' he had asked one of his daughters very recently. 'Thursday,' she said. But that Thursday Sandra did not take her evening off; instead she went down to the kitchen to make a cup of tea for herself and Lucan's estranged wife. Sandra was bashed and bludgeoned. She was stuffed into a sack. Bashed also was Lucan's wife when she came down to see what was the matter. She was bashed and bloodied. She told how she had at last foiled the attacker whom she named as her husband. She bit him; she had got him by the balls, unmanned him, offered to do a deal of complicity with him and then, when he went to the bathroom to wash away the blood, slipped out of the house and staggered a few yards down the street to a pub into which she burst, covered with blood. 'Murder! . . . the children are still in the house . . .'

He had tried to choke her with a gloved hand and to finish her with the same blunt instrument by which Sandra was killed.

The police arrived at the house. The Earl had fled. He had telephoned his mother telling her to take care of the children, which she did, that very night.

The Earl was known to have been seen briefly by a friend. Then lost. Smuggled out of the country or dead by his own hand?

The good Dr Wolf looked at her patient and let the above facts run through her head. Was this man sitting in front of her, the claimant to be Lord Lucan, in fact the missing murder suspect? He was smiling, smiling away at her thoughtfulness. And what had he to smile about?

She could ring Interpol, but had private reasons not to do so.

She said, 'There is another "Lord Lucan" in Paris at the moment. I wonder which of you is the real one? Anyway, our time is up. I will be away tomorrow. Come on Friday.'

'Another *Lucan*?'

'I will see you on Friday.'

2

Hildegard weighed up the odds between the two claimants while she ate her lunch at her favourite bistro in the rue du Dragon. She was eating tripe, their speciality. And what, she wondered, did Lucky mean by a pact with the Devil? She might bring him round to this. Whether he was the real Lord Lucan or not, Hildegard felt he was referring to something genuinely in his past. She would not be at all surprised to find that, as the missing Earl, he was a fake; but she would be astonished if he had not at some earlier time compromised his conscience: 'I sold my soul to the Devil.' That must mean something.

Walker, the name by which her other Lucan patient had asked to be called, had an appointment with Hildegard two days later. Walker was a surname; his first name, Robert, was never used. 'Robert Walker. Please always call me Walker. Nobody must guess that I am the seventh Earl of Lucan. There is a warrant out for my arrest.' Walker was tall, white-haired, white-moustached. From the newspaper photographs dating back twenty-odd years, he might well be the missing Earl, and again, he might not.

'On the whole,' said Hildegard, 'I think he is not Lucan. And neither is the other, most probably.' She was talking to her companion-in-life (as he had been for over five years) Jean-Pierre Roget. They sat in the sitting-room, part of their large flat. It was evening. She sat in a beige leather armchair, and so did he.

'Undoubtedly,' he said, 'the two men are acquainted with each other, working together. It would be too much to ask that they should separately consult you among all the psychiatrists in Paris, two imposters, or one an imposter, one real. I can't believe it.'

'Nor can I,' she said. 'Nor do I.'

'You should try to keep an open mind.'

'What does that mean?' she said.

'At least listen well to what they say.'

'I've listened to Walker. He sounds very troubled.'

'It's taken him a long time to be troubled. What has he been doing all these years not to be troubled before?' Jean-Pierre wondered aloud.

'Escaping from justice. Running away here and there. He had friends.'

'And Interpol? How does he know you won't hand him over?'

'Neither of them knows,' she said. 'That's what I can't understand.'

'Oh,' he said, 'I can. People generally have faith in the discretion of a psychiatrist, as they do with a priest.'

'Professionally, I was quite happy working with Walker,' she said. 'But now, with this new one . . . Sooner or later I'll have to come to grips with him.'

'What does he call himself?'

'Lucan,' she said. 'Just that.'

'What do his friends call him?'

'He says he's called Lucky. His friends have always called him Lucky Lucan. That was in the papers.'

'Which of your two patients,' said Jean-Pierre, 'resembles his photographs most?'

'Both of them,' said Hildegard.

'Hildegard,' he said, 'could either of them have anything on you? Something from your past, anything?'

'Oh, my God,' she said. 'There is always that possibility. Anyone any time could have something in their past. I can't think . . . but it would be unlikely, unbelievable. What would such people want with my past?'

'Perhaps nothing,' he said.

'Perhaps – what do you mean, Jean-Pierre?'

'Well, I don't mean exactly that you yourself might be wanted by Interpol. On the other hand . . .'

'On the other hand, what?' She had become uneasy, menacing. Jean-Pierre decided to back off.

'There is no other hand,' he said, 'since you are not on the wanted list.' He smiled very fetchingly at her. His affection was real. 'If one of these men is the missing Lucan he might feel it safe to confide in you if he knew of something in your past life that you wanted to hide. But as that is not so, since you say it isn't, that theory is ruled out, isn't it?'

'No,' she said. 'If one of them is the real Lucan he might imagine that he had something on me. Anyone might get that idea. They are probably in it together, is all I say.'

3

Walker kept his appointment with Hildegard.

'I am not really interested in whether you are Lord Lucan or not,' she told him. 'I am interested in you, what you are doing here, why you need a psychiatrist, why your nerve has failed you if that is so. I am interested in a number of important factors, but not greatly in what your name may have been in 1974. You are prompted to see me now, in these weeks. Why?'

'In England,' he said, 'I have been declared officially dead in order to wind up my estate. I have come to think of myself as a dead man. It distresses me.'

'It is believed by some people,' she said, 'that the real Lord Lucan committed suicide shortly after he had murdered a girl over twenty years ago. It is a rational belief.'

'His body was never found,' said Walker. 'Naturally. Because I am Lucan.'

'You are not the only claimant,' she said.

'Really? Who is the other?'

'There could be many others. Several, at least. At what scope or advantage I can't imagine. I should have thought you'd want to keep it quiet.'

'I am keeping it quiet,' said Walker. 'My secret is safe with you.'

'Are you sure?'

'Yes, I'm sure.'

'I have only to ring Interpol.'

'So have I.'

'To give yourself up?' she said.

'No, to give you up, Dr Wolf.'

'Me? What do you mean?' Her voice had changed as if she had difficulty swallowing, as if her mouth was dry.

'You are Beate Pappenheim, the fake stigmatic from Bavaria who was exposed in 1986, who disappeared with so many millions of marks from the Pappenheim Catholic Fund that nobody knew how many, who –'

'What you are saying,' she said, 'means nothing to me. Let's return to your problem, which, as I see it, is one of identity.'

'I know who I am,' he said. 'I have friends. Helpers. People who know who I am.'

'Perhaps, then, you don't need me,' she said, arranging the pens on her desk a little more neatly than they had been.

'Beate Pappenheim,' he said, 'how long does a warrant for arrest last? A whole lifetime?'

'My name is not Pappenheim,' she said, 'and I am not a lawyer. I imagine a warrant for arrest in most countries lasts a lifetime or until the event of an arrest being made, but surely among your friends and helpers there is one who knows or practises criminal law?'

'My friends are getting old and some have died,' said Walker the so-called Lucan. 'None of them has practised the law. They are gentlemen, they are millionaires, but not lawyers.'

'You come here,' said Dr Wolf, 'with your story of being Robert Walker alias the seventh Earl of Lucan, a fugitive from British law, wanted for murder. What proof can you offer that any of this story is true?'

'I don't need to prove anything.'

'If you wish to continue as my patient you do,' she said. 'Especially since I have another patient, Lucan, who also claims that he did the murder; in fact, is almost proud of it.'

'Dr Pappenheim . . .'

'Mr Walker, it's money you want, isn't it?'

'Partly.'

'Bring me proof that you are Lucan and I'll pay you, partly. And now your time is up, for which you pay me. You pay at the desk and no fooling.'

'Next Friday, Dr Pappenheim?'

'Get out.' She glared at him but he smiled at her as he rose, suave, casually dressed, rich, manicured, simply awful.

Hildegard took out of her handbag a small scent-spray which she puffed on either side of her neck. She put the spray back in her bag, thinking, I'm an animal trying to put that man off the scent. Where did he come from, that muck-raker? She phoned Jean-Pierre, knowing confidently of his admiration for her methods and his respect for her fame. 'Yes, I am being threatened,' she said, 'about some past life of mine, something in another world. It's upsetting me. Not rationally, of course. But I don't know quite what to do.'

'We can discuss it tonight, Hildegard. Why are you upset? Don't you expect your patients to be nuts?'

'It's that first Lord Lucan, Walker by name. Who do you suppose Walker really is?'

'A private detective,' said Jean-Pierre. 'Someone making enquiries about the real Lucan, it could be.'

'See you later,' she said.

Jean-Pierre was seven years her junior. Their difference in age was not apparent. Hildegard had a charming face and form, with dark well-cared-for hair, a pale skin and large grey eyes. Jean-Pierre was a man of big build, already grisly-grey with a beard. For over five years now he had shared his life with Hildegard. He could think of no one else, practically nothing else, but Hildegard.

Jean-Pierre was a metal- and wood-worker, with a workshop and foundry where he spent his working days. Jean-Pierre had a genius for making things, such as bells, fire-irons, horse brasses, doors, windows, and especially adjustable bookcases. He also restored objects which had been broken; he made lamps out of vases and mended good china jugs. His workshop was like a junk heap of Europe, a history of antiquity, with its corner cabinets and consoles filled and littered with little boxes, primitive telephones, shells, ancient coins, everything. He used coins for eyes, frequently, when he felt in the mood to make up a mask in wood and iron. He liked wooden shoe-forms. This place of business was in the suburbs, by road (he had a Fiat van) half an hour from the centre outside of the rush hour. He now lived with Hildegard in the rue du Dragon on the left bank.

4

Do not lose hold of the name Hildegard Wolf. Her real name, Beate Pappenheim, now comes into this story, but she leads us inevitably to Hildegard. Beate was a young student in Munich in the 'seventies when she suddenly got tired, very, very tired, of being poor. This happens to a great number of impoverished people. Not all can do something about that condition.

Beate, a medical student who hoped to specialise in feminist psychology, was having a very hard time. She attended her university classes in the mornings and early afternoon she studied English. But from four p.m. to eight p.m. she had to work a four-hour shift at the handbag counter of a department store. It was the only way she could make a living, earning enough to pay for her cheap bedsitting room and meagre food. Her parents lived in the country on a pig farm. She went to see them by bus one weekend a month, taking with her an offering of tinned foods, oatmeal, or pickled cucumber. Her studies fascinated her. The job at the handbag department of the store wearied her heart out. She was tired of women who came to buy handbags and who tried the capacity of their purchases by first emptying their own bags to see if the contents would fit into the new one. It was then that Beate Pappenheim would frequently catch sight of the fat, bulging notecases of some of these women. Sometimes the money, solid packets of Deutschmarks, was not even enclosed in a wallet. Beate coveted this money. She would have stolen had she been able to do so without detection. She was tired, tired. Still in her twenties, she felt worn out. Her need for money was continual. Her boy-friend was a theological student, of the Protestant faith. He spoke English fluently, made her speak to him in English so that she could read the English-language text-books in psychology. He would have loved to be a Catholic, the churches were so much more cheerful than any others, so full of colour and glitter, incense and images.

One day on a Saturday when she was not visiting the farm, her boyfriend, Heinrich, came to visit her. It was three in the afternoon. He had a key. He found her on the bed covered in blood. She was having a menstrual haemorrhage. Blood all over the sheets, the floor, her hands. Heinrich ran for the landlady, who screamed when she saw Beate. Meanwhile the young man located a doctor who came and gave Beate an injection and the landlady orders to clean up the mess. Heinrich took over the job from the trembling woman who was also concerned about her bed sheets and the curtains, for blood had even spread to the windows, somehow.

Much later Beate was able to sit up. The landlady, to Beate's surprise, was now sympathetic and brought her some soup which Heinrich heated up on the spirit stove in the corner of the room. 'You reminded me,' said the landlady, who was a Catholic, 'of a picture I saw as a child of Sister Anastasia of the Five Wounds. She was a stigmatic. She worked miracles, so they said. But the Church never recognised her as a saint. When the Bishop came to visit the churches in the diocese we had to run and put the picture out of sight. But we often had a collection for Sister Anastasia. She was good to the poor.'

This was how Beate got her idea of being a holy stigmatic. She changed her address. Every monthly menstrual cycle she covered herself in blood and bandaged her hands so that blood appeared to seep through. She was stricken every month, as the phenomenon is traditionally represented, with at least one of the five wounds of Christ (a nail-wound on each hand and foot, and a sword wound in the side). In between the cycles she wrote out testimonies to her healing powers, aided and abetted by Heinrich who appeared so much to believe in Beate's claims that possibly, on interrogation, it would have emerged that he truly believed them. The nature of belief is very strange.

Beate had arranged for thousands of leaflets to be printed:

BLESSED BEATE PAPPENHEIM

THE STIGMATIC OF MUNICH

Please repeat the following prayer seven mornings a week for seven weeks. Beate Pappenheim prays and suffers for you.

O Lord, bless us through the good offices of our sister Beate Pappenheim. We beseech Thee to hear her prayer on behalf of our sick/suffering brother/sister [delete as appropriate] N. In the name of the Five Wounds of Jesus Christ Our Lord.

Underneath was a picture of Beate holding up her blood-stained hands.

Below this was printed a brief biography of Beate with emphasis on her church-going persistence from childhood upwards.

The leaflet concluded:

I enclose the sum of . . . . for the aid of Beate
Pappenheim's Poor. Please send what you can afford. No
gift is too small.

Heinrich had some friends in the theological college on
whom he tried this leaflet. 'She really works miracles.' Nearly
all of them laughed it off. But not all. After a while the news
of Beate's miracle-working reached the nursing profession
and somehow or other got to the shores of Ireland, the great
land of believers. There it exploded into a real cult, so that
when eventually (it took eight years) she was exposed as a
fraud by analysis of her menstrual blood, more money in
Irish currency than any other was found to have been placed
to her account. Meanwhile, she had escaped, disappeared.

Beate during that time had been able to live in comfort.
Every month she took to her bed and bloodily received
pilgrims. Miracles did happen, as in fact they sometimes
do. When she was finally exposed, a great number of her
followers, mainly poor people, refused to believe what the
newspapers reported.

Beate herself had fled abroad. She changed her name to
Hildegard Wolf. She moved, later, to Paris and set up as a
psychiatrist there. With her change of name her personality
expanded; it changed considerably. She would have sworn
that the Beate Pappenheim of her past was a 'different
person' from herself; but she had never for the past twelve
years been obliged to consider the question. She had just
put Beate out of her mind, destroying her old birth certificate and replacing it with a new one obtained from a lawyer
in Marseilles.

She had not been forgotten altogether by the acquaintances, the friends, enemies and hangers-on of her old life,
those who had profited by the cult of Blessed Beate

Pappenheim. And many a poor and ageing Catholic devotee of France and the British Isles remembered her name, remembered the sacrifices of their youth – the small sums, to them large, sent to Germany each month in the form of postal orders, or simple ten-shilling notes put into an envelope with a prayerful letter. Because they had sent the money they mostly continued to believe in her, long after the *Catholic Herald* and *The Tablet*, for instance, had published reports of Beate's scientifically proved fraud. 'Beate, you have got to be true. I believe in you because I sent you all my savings and I prayed your Novena' were the words of one typical letter subsequently Returned to Sender, Address Unknown. Heinrich returned to his theological college, keeping quiet.

Walker, the first so-called Lord Lucan, arrived in time for his next appointment, and was shown in. He sat down and lit a cigarette without permission.

'Put it out,' she said.

'I like a cigarette after lunch.'

'But I haven't had my lunch,' said Hildegard firmly. 'I am just about to send down to the brasserie for a sandwich.' She buzzed her secretary. 'Have them send up a ham-and-cheese sandwich and a quarter bottle of red wine,' she ordered.

'To get down to the question of your identity . . .' Walker began. But Hildegard was defiant. 'If you have come here for a consultation that is what you'll get. On the question of sandwiches, sooner or later we all have to stop for a sandwich or grab a sandwich before the theatre. I always have a sandwich sent up on days like today when one is expecting a boring patient, very boring. Neither in anticipation, nor retrospect, can one's digestion cope with a full meal. It is best to *faire monter* a sandwich. How old are you?'

'Sixty-five next December.'

'You look older.'

'I've had a rough time. I've been on the run. Let me explain –'

'When I've had my sandwich.' Hildegard kept silent till the girl had arrived bearing a tray. She started to eat. Between mouthfuls she spoke on, but every time she took a bite he tried to speak, too. It was quite a battle, and Hildegard won it. 'Sandwiches,' she said, 'like diamonds, are for ever. Children love them. They are the most useful, yet often the most despised of foods.' She was carried away by fantasy. 'My fondest memories from childhood are connected with sandwiches. At children's parties –'

'The most secure way of keeping my identity private is not to reveal it. But if I do have to make it known that I am Lucan, as in the case of consulting a psychiatrist as you see I have decided to do,' he said, 'the only secure way is to know something secret about the psychiatrist equal in criminality to my own case.'

'Murder would be difficult to equal,' she said. 'The sandwich was first invented by the fourth Earl of Sandwich in the eighteenth century who was a gambler like yourself, if in fact you are Lord Lucan. He devised this means of nourishment at odd hours without the necessity of leaving the gaming table for his meals, Mr Walker.'

'But you are still wanted for fraud,' said Mr Walker, 'of a particularly disreputable kind. How many poor housemaids did you rob of their savings when you were Beate Pappenheim?'

'Where you come from, of course,' said Hildegard, 'the sandwiches are spread with butter. Sandwiches of the British Isles differ greatly from German sandwiches.' She poured herself a glass of wine from the small bottle on the tray.

There remained another sandwich which she lifted and slowly contemplated, then carefully took a nibble of. 'German sandwiches are much thicker, with some sort of pickles and sausage or cheese inside. Your English sandwiches, on the other hand, are cut thin, thin. They are buttered. They have fillings like chopped egg and tomatoes, sprinkled with cress which hangs in tiny threads, temptingly, out of the sides. They –'

'I know, I know,' said Walker. 'I remember them at the school sports occasions. What I have come here to discuss is the situation, which is, what are you going to do about it? I refer to the situation I described at our last sitting.'

'Oh, you are growing a beard,' Hildegard said, 'and besides,' she said as she sipped and daintily chewed at her leisure, 'there are shrimps, there are lobster and salmon, which make ideal sandwich-fillings. Strawberry sandwiches are great for picnics.

'There was a time,' she continued before Mr Walker could interrupt again, 'when bakers would sell a sandwich loaf already sliced, either white, brown or wholemeal. Probably there remain some bakers who do this. Now, I'm sure that while you sit there you find yourself eagerly desiring one of these delicious sandwiches. Don't they fill you with English nostalgia?' She wiped the corners of her mouth delicately with the pink paper napkin provided by the brasserie, and looked at her watch.

'Goodness – the time!' she said. 'I'm afraid we have to make it an abbreviated session today as I have a most urgent engagement outside the office with a patient too sick to visit me. I must visit her. Please make another appointment at the desk, if you wish to continue. Next Friday?'

'No,' he said.

'Very well,' she said. 'Good-bye.'

'You'll be hearing from me,' said Mr Walker alias Lord Lucan. 'I'll be in touch, Fräulein Pappenheim.'

She had pressed the buzzer on her desk. The petite receptionist appeared at the door.

'The patient wishes to make another appointment,' said Hildegard. She added in a more confiding tone, 'The usual fee.'

5

From all accounts and police records of the affair of the seventh Earl of Lucan he was an extremely arrogant person. Arrogance is incurable. It usually arises from a deep (sometimes justified) sense of inferiority. Another feature of this Earl of Lucan, which supposedly he maintained, was a peculiar eating habit which lasted apparently the whole of his adult life up to his disappearance. And beyond? He ate nothing but smoked salmon and lamb chops every day; in winter the chops were grilled, in summer they were served *en gelée*. Dull people found him amusing. Interesting people thought him desperately dull. His wife was not very popular with Lucan's gambling set. Lady Lucan was unimaginative but honest. She protected her children, and in a bitter court case with Lucan she had won custody of them.

Jean-Pierre had studied the huge pile of press-cuttings which Hildegard had obtained from London. He said to her, 'The two Lucans are in league, you may be sure of that, if one of them is trying in some way to blackmail you. Myself, I think it unlikely that two men should turn up at your studio at the same time, both claiming to be Lucans.'

'I think the second may be the genuine man,' said Hildegard, 'the first a friend of his, a helper, making sure I don't turn the genuine Lucan over to the police.'

'I am not sure of that,' he said.

'Nor am I. Perhaps neither man is Lucan.'

'Beate Pappenheim. Was it really your name?'

'Yes.'

'Beate Pappenheim . . . how lovely.'

'Why,' said Jean-Pierre the following evening, 'did you not tell me before about your exciting early life as a stigmatic?'

'Listen,' she said, 'I caused miracles. I really did cure some people. Strangely enough, I did.'

'I believe you,' said Jean-Pierre. He thought: I do believe her. She is magic. And when he thought of his life previous to meeting Hildegard he wondered how he had managed.

'We could put one of your Lucans to the test by asking him to dinner. Give him smoked salmon followed by lamb chops and see if perhaps he eats them eagerly. It says in all the books about him that he ate just that and only that,' Jean-Pierre said.

'If you prepared the meal he would of course eat it eagerly,' she said. Jean-Pierre was indeed a good cook and sometimes made their dinner on the nights-off of their two *au pair* young men. 'Which one should we invite, Lucan I or Lucan II?' said Hildegard.

'Lucan II alias Lucky.'

'That's what I'll do. Invite Lucky and give him smoked salmon and lamb chops. That diet of his was a detail reported in all the books and articles about him. It would be of some interest to see how he reacts. I'd like to make him nervous. Perhaps I could ask him a question like "Suppose that Death is a male character, what would Death's wife be like?" '

'From what I've read about him, that's too imaginative. He could never grasp such a proposition.'

'Perhaps not,' she said. 'In fact I am sure you're right. Do you know he's reputed to be very, very dull?'

'Yes, I know that. Perhaps I could lace his drink with something – we'll see. I could get you a harmless loquacious pill,' Jean-Pierre suggested. 'Something to last the evening and at the same time make him talk. I know a pharmacist.'

'How clever you are!'

Hildegard thought this over all the next day. The more she thought of it the more she liked the idea of a pill secretly administered to aid the patient to speak out. Unethical, of course. Illegal, no doubt. Neither of the lords had hitherto bothered Hildegard personally very much, nor did they do so now. She only wondered how she could achieve a good result . . . 'I could get you a loquacious pill . . .' She really adored Jean-Pierre; he was so very much of her own calibre. If you can comprehend a morality devoid of ethics or civil law, this was really the guiding principle of both people. And in their dealings with Lord Lucan it was on those particular moral grounds that they determined to deal with him heavily. What shocked Hildegard most in the Lucan story was his, and his set's, lack of remorse over the dead nanny, a young girl of twenty-nine, full of prettiness, life, humour. When a relative called at the Lucan home by arrangement to collect her belongings, they were handed over at the door by Lady Lucan herself, stuffed into a paper bag, and that was that.

Hildegard and Jean-Pierre read through all the press-cuttings together. 'What strikes me,' said Jean-Pierre, 'is how Lucan succeeded in antagonising the police and the press without ever meeting them. This was mainly due, I think, to the attitude of his friends.'

'But he was really an awful man,' said Hildegard. 'For one thing he was sexually violent. He beat his wife with a cane. Very sick, that.'

'He was sick, yes. All big gamblers are sick, anyway. And if he was also a sexual sadist . . . do you recognise any of that in either of your men?'

'I see it in both. The possibility is in both. The evidence in the law suit for his children shattered Lucan. He thought his wife would observe secrecy in the matter of his sexual sadism, but she didn't. He felt betrayed. But as he was trying to make her out to be mad, obviously she had a moral right to reveal his mental condition. Besides, a bad-tempered man looking after children . . .'

'I suppose,' said Jean-Pierre, 'you realise that, unlike most of your patients, the authentic Lord Lucan really is mad?'

'You think so?'

'I'm convinced. On the facts revealed in the inquest and the biographical research over the years, he is insane.'

'But which one is the real one?'

'Hildegard, I don't like your being alone with him. Are you sure you are safe – I mean, physically?'

'I'm sure of nothing.'

'Except that Lucan I, Walker, is trying to threaten you, to obtain your complicity through blackmail. For which,' said Jean-Pierre, 'I will somehow smooth him out, I will solve his problem.'

'Darling, he is very large.'

'And I, too. I am also clever.'

Lucky had consumed his smoked salmon, served as it had been with very fine slices of buttered toast. He was now working his way through the three lamb chops on his plate. The wine was from Bordeaux and he absorbed it like blotting paper.

'What was remarkable,' he said, 'was that there was so much blood. If I had got my wife as I thought I was doing,

26

there would never have been so much blood, so much. But I will never forget the blood that flowed in such quantity from that girl, Sandra Rivett. There must be something about the lower orders, they bleed so. I cannot forget that blood. It got everywhere. Pools of it.'

They had decided to dine in a bistro, to give Jean-Pierre time to focus his full attention on Lucky. All round the walls were signed photographs of old-time actors wearing hats, and actresses greatly be-furred. Hildegard found these reassuring, they pre-dated the memories both of her guest and of herself, and were something solid to be surrounded by in this moment of testing and confessing. 'Blood,' she said, 'is nothing new to me. As you probably know.'

'I should probably know?'

'Yes, your accomplice, the other Lucan, has no doubt informed you that I was the stigmatic of Munich, Beate Pappenheim.'

'I seem to remember the name,' said Lucky. 'But I have no accomplice. Are you crazy? My information comes from the late Reverend Brother Heinrich in whose prayer-hostel I lodged for some months.'

'I was covered with blood, endless blood. And I effected countless cures. I am not crazy. Heinrich was a poor little student. He took my money, plenty of it.'

'There was a scandal, though, I seem to think.'

'You seem to think right. I am wanted for fraud as you are for murder. Heinrich knew that I changed my name.'

'Murder plus attempted murder,' he said. 'My wife didn't bleed so much, you know. It was the nanny. Blood all over the place.'

Hildegard felt almost sympathetic towards him. 'Blood,' she said, 'blood.'

'They say it is purifying,' he said.

She thought, immediately, 'Could he be a religious maniac?'

'It is not purifying,' she said, 'it is sticky. We are never washed by blood.'

'It is said we are washed in the Blood of the Lamb,' he said, sticking his knife into lamb chop number three. 'I sang in the school choir.'

She was exultant in her suspicion. A religious maniac. The possibility consoled her. She had not, after all, found the clear opportunity of slipping Jean-Pierre's talking pill into his wine but still Lucky was talking, talking. She assumed it was the psychological effect on him of his old menu, salmon and lamb, which in fact he must have been deprived of for most of his clandestinity, lest the police should be on the watch for just that clue.

6

Generally speaking, Scotswomen who do not dye their hair have a homogeneous island-born look, a well-born look, which does not apply in the south. The man who called himself Lucky Lucan, who was a snob from his deepest guts, sat with his whisky and water in the lounge of the Golf Hotel at a small village outside Aberdeen, and greatly admired the young fair good-boned waitress. He had picked this spot, as he always picked spots when it was time for him to move on, with a pin on a map open before him. It had always worked well. Nobody was looking for him at a place he had picked out with his eyes shut and a pin in his hand. This time he had, however, picked from a map of North Britain. He had business there.

'Christina,' she said when he asked the girl her name. 'Do you want a table for lunch?'

'I do. And I don't suppose,' he said, 'that you have smoked salmon or lamb chops on the menu?'

'We have both.'

'Good. I like lamb chops.'

He was not really aware of the fact that he was sizing up the girl in a certain way that related to Hildegard Wolf. She was younger than Hildegard. Her hair was light gold. She was decidedly skinnier. Lucky then realised, all of a sudden, that he was really thinking of Hildegard, and had been all through his nine holes of golf.

'What is your name?' he said again to the Scottish waitress.

'Christina. They call me Kirsty.'

'Kirsty, I want a double malt whisky. I want smoked salmon to start followed by lamb chops and the trimmings.'

'Your room number?' she said.

'I'll pay the restaurant bill in cash.'

He paid everything in cash, on principle. His source of cash was here in Britain. Nowadays, he came twice a year to collect it personally from his old friend, rich Benny Rolfe, who always, since Lucky's operation to change his features, had a fat package of money ready for him on his visits. Benny on this occasion was abroad, but he had arranged for the package of pounds sterling to be placed in Lucky's hands, as he had done twice a year since 1974 without fail. Most of the cash came out of Benny's own pocket, but there was always a certain amount contributed by Lucan's other old friends and collected by Benny Rolfe.

'Aren't you disgusted, ever, by what I did?' Lucky had asked Benny on one of these occasions. 'Aren't any of you horrified? Because, when I look back on it, I'm horrified myself.'

'No, dear fellow, it was a bungle like any other bungle. You should never let a bungle weigh on your conscience.'

'But if I'd killed my wife?'

'That would not have been a bungle. You would not have been the unlucky one.'

'I think of Nanny Rivett. She had an awful lot of blood. Pints, quarts of it. The blood poured out, all over the place. I was wading in it in the dark. Didn't you read about the blood in the papers?'

'I did, to tell you the truth. Perhaps murdered nannies have more blood to spill than the upper class, do you think?'

'Exactly what I would say,' Lucan had said. He was disappointed that Benny himself was not available on this visit. He ate through his lamb chops. He studied Kirsty and compared her to Hildegard. From the window of the dining room the North Sea spread its great apparent calm. Benny Rolfe was now in his mid-seventies. Nearly all Lucky's old staunch aiders and abetters were over seventy now. Who would provide him with money when his benefactors were gone? So mused Lucky, never letting his mind embrace an obvious fact: one of these days he, too, would be 'gone': a solution to the cash problem. But Lucky did not think along those lines, and he was now filled with nostalgia for Hildegard that dear doctor. 'We are washed in the Blood of the Lamb.' He looked warily over his shoulder at this thought.

After dinner he went for a stroll, stopping at a little arts-and-crafts shop which was open late, precisely for people like Lucky to stop at. Among the hideous Scottish folk-jewellery he found a fine piece of carved crystal, a pendant, for Hildegard, for Hildegard. He waited while the bearded young fellow wrapped it up for Hildegard, paid over the price and tucked the little parcel in his breast pocket.

7

All along the shelves under the three windows of Hildegard's consulting room was placed her collection of miniature cactus plants. It was of such an extreme rarity that Hildegard was quite annoyed when one of her patients innocently presented her with another cactus. It was never of an equally rare status as her own ones, and yet she was obliged to have the new little plant on show at least for a while.

Walker had brought her such a plant; it was good but not quite good enough. She placed it with pleased carefulness on the shelf, quite as if it was of the last rarity.

Hildegard waved Walker to his chair.

'There are two of you,' Hildegard said.

Walker looked put out. 'Oh, there has to be two of us,' said Walker. 'One who committed the crime and one who didn't.'

'And which of the two is the real Lucan?'

'I am,' he said. His eyes shifted from the window to the door as if entrapped.

'Well, you're a liar,' she said.

'I often wonder about that,' said Walker. 'After years of being me, it's difficult, now, to conceive being him. How did you know there was a pretender?'

'A man called Lucky Lucan is one of my clients. He claims to be the seventh Earl.'

'What a sneak, what a rotter!' Walker was really upset. 'The seventh Earl is myself.'

'Sneaks and rotters hack children's nurses to death, you mean?'

'It was a mistake. Nanny Rivett was killed in error.'

'And the hack-and-bash job on Lady Lucan?'

'That was different. She should have died. I was in debt.'

'God, I'd like to turn you over to Interpol,' said Hildegard.

'You won't do that, Beate Pappenheim. Don't forget that I'm a professional gambler. I know when the odds are loaded against me. That's why I'm on the run, that's why I'm here, in fact. All I am asking for, Beate Pappenheim, is free psychiatric treatment. Nothing more. Just that. Your secret, your bloody secret will be safe with me if mine remains safe with you.'

'And Lucky Lucan – my other client?'

'He shouldn't have come to you at all. He's a swine.'

'He looks awfully like the original.' Hildegard opened the file she had already placed on her desk in preparation for the interview. 'See here,' she said, 'Lucan aged thirty-eight on the beach, Lucan in his ermine robes, Lucan in his tennis clothes, Lucan at a dance, and playing cards at the Clermont Club with his notorious friends. And,' she said, 'I have also a photo-kit of what he should look like now, based on computer-devised photos of his parents at your age, and here's another police identikit which allows for plastic adaptations to the jawbone and the nose. Look at it. Look.'

'But look at me.'

'You look the same height. Your eyes are spaced convincingly. Your English voice is very probable. Yes, but you don't convince me. How did you get together with Lucky Lucan?'

'I hired him. There were so many occasions when I was

nearly caught, especially when collecting the funds that my friends have put at my disposal, that I thought I would take on a double. He effectively fools my friends when he goes to collect. Strangely enough Lucky, so-called, resembles me when I was in my forties more than he does now. And of course, they hardly want him to linger.'

'And suppose it's the other way round? My other client is Lucan and you are the hired substitute?'

'No,' said Walker.

'Well, I can't take you both on as patients.'

'You won't need to. I'll deal with Lucky, so-called. People like us know how to deal with people like him.'

These last words of that afternoon's conversation hovered over Hildegard's imagination. '*People like us know how to deal* . . .' Of course Walker had meant to disturb her. She was aware of that. Once before he had said, when she had asked him why he had not taken the simpler course of giving himself up and standing trial for murder, 'People like us don't go to prison.' He was over-full of his aristocratic qualities, as he supposed them to be, and this was what had led Hildegard to assume he was a fake. 'People like us *know how to deal with people like him.*' Perhaps, after all, he was the real Lord Lucan. '*People like us know how to deal* . . .' Did Lucan have that conviction in mind when he 'dealt' with the woman he thought was his wife, when he 'dealt' with the knowledge of his blunder that he had killed only the children's nurse? People like us . . . people like them . . . It was almost melodramatic, but then, as Hildegard told Jean-Pierre that night, the very situation of Lord Lucan and his disappearance had a melodramatic touch. It was this very naïve approach to his personal drama that had probably confused the police in the days after the murder. They were looking for upper-class sophistication, but they got nothing but cheap show-biz from Lucan's friends. Lucan had been drinking heavily, Lucan was hopelessly in debt. But no, Lucan is a friend of ours, he is one of us and you don't understand that people like us . . . Lucan had sent letters to a friend while he was still so covered in blood that the stains appeared on the envelope. Lucan had turned up in a panic at a friend's house that night of the murder, with a bloodstain on his trousers.

Blood. 'What I'm afraid of,' Hildegard said when she discussed it with her lover, 'is that Walker will murder Lucky. It would be in character.'

'But you say that you believe Lucky to be the real Lucan?'

'There is always a doubt. I could be wrong. But Walker sticks in my mind as an unscrupulous fake.'

Jean-Pierre had been making notes. It was an hour before they would sit down to dinner. Jean-Pierre gave Hildegard her preferred drink, a small quantity of whisky dowsed in water, took one for himself, a dry martini, and got out his notebook. He read:

After twenty-five years of playing the part of the missing Lord Lucan he surely is the part. The operative word is 'missing'. If indeed he has been Lord Lucan in an earlier life he had never gone missing before. After the murder he went without money apparently, without decent clothing, without a passport. He just disappeared.

If he was the real Lord Lucan the clandestine life must have meant a loss of innocence – that he had not known he possessed. The spontaneous pleasure, for instance, of just being in Paris, as so many English people experience. The boulevards, the banks of the Seine, the traffic, the bistros, the graffiti on the walls – all lost in the new life of careful watchfulness. The odds would be against him, as he must have known if he was Lucan the professional gambler. The police were active in those early months of his clandestine flight.

And as the years piled up with nothing achieved but his furtive travels in South America, in Africa, in Asia, between intervals of quick, dangerous trips to Scotland and Paris to pick up his old friends' money, what had he become? Someone untraceable with blood on his hands, in his head, in his memory. Blood . . .

. . . My nature is subdued
To what it works in, like the dyer's hand.

When he disappeared in 1974 he was thirty-nine. The detective assigned to his case, Roy Ranson, died in recent years. Sightings of the seventh Earl are still frequent. Lucan is here, he is there, he is everywhere. In a final message to Lucan, Roy Ranson wrote, 'Keep a watchful eye over your shoulder. There will always be someone looking for Lucan.'

He must have gone through several false passports, several false names.

'Well, Hildegard,' said Jean-Pierre, 'which of your Lucans fits my profile best?'

'Neither,' she said, 'and both.'

'Why,' said Jean-Pierre, 'are the Lucans getting psychiatric therapy?'

'They are sick,' said Hildegard. 'Especially Lucky. Sick, and he knows it.'

'I mean to find out,' said Jean-Pierre, 'why they actually want psychiatric treatment.'

'Perhaps they need money. They want it from me,' said

Hildegard. 'It could be that Lucan's source of income is drying up.'

'It could be. I'd like to know,' said Jean-Pierre. 'I read a recent article in which Lucan's friends claim that he is dead beyond the shadow of a doubt. "Shadow of a doubt" were the words. If they never found his body or other evidence there is a shadow, there is a doubt. There is a possibility that he is alive and another possibility that he is dead. There is no "beyond the shadow of a doubt". None whatsoever. That is journalistic talk. There are shadows; there are doubts.'

'That's what I thought when I read it. Not that I care one way or another. Only I have these Lucan patients and I'm under pressure of, well, call it exposure.'

'Yes, I call it exposure, Hildegard. Let's be clear. One gets nowhere by being muddy.'

'Nowhere,' she said, smiling gratefully at him.

Their dinner was prepared and served by the two *au pair* young men who were close friends with each other. It was a convenient arrangement. Dick and Paul were former students at a psychiatric institution where Hildegard lectured. She had found them to be engrossed with each other, anxious to shed their families, and not at all keen to study. They were delighted to show their prowess at cooking (which was not very great) and general housekeeping. They got on well with Hildegard and in a chummy way with the maid Olivia, who came every morning to clean up. Dick and Paul went shopping for the household, and advised Olivia how to shop economically for her sexy clothes. It was a tranquil background for the love affair between Hildegard and Jean-Pierre. Only the facts of blood which hovered over Hildegard's professional life and her memories of the past disturbed her.

The dinner consisted of a mysterious brown fish soup, a mousse of spinach and cream cheese with tiny new potatoes, and a peach ice-cream with cherry sauce. Jean-Pierre and Hildegard ate it appreciatively, half-consciously, happier with the fact of being cooked for and served at all than with the actual dinner. The young men, slim, tall and wiry, cleared the table and brought them coffee in the sitting-room. It had been arranged at first that their status entitled them to join Hildegard and Jean-Pierre at the table for meals, but really they preferred to eat alone together in the kitchen, with occasional friends who had belonged to their student days, rather than with their employers. And this suited Jean-Pierre and Hildegard, too. They could talk more openly, for one thing.

While they dined they discussed that other supper in the bistro with Lucky. He had certainly consumed his smoked salmon followed by lamb chops with obvious satisfaction.

'Well, it was very good smoked salmon; the lamb chops were very well prepared.'

'What did you make of him?'

'From the way he was talking I would say Lucky is Lucan, and his mind is giving up. His conscience is taking over. In his mind, God might tell him to kill again.'

Walker appeared in Jean-Pierre's workshop. There were no customers at that hour, ten-thirty a.m. Jean-Pierre was working on a plastic eye which was intended for a statue.

'My name is Walker.'

'I know who you are.'

'I want to speak to you,' Walker told Jean-Pierre.

'I have no money for you,' said Jean-Pierre.

Walker left the premises.

*

Hildegard was in her office talking to the patient known as Lucky.

'I'm not supposed to be here,' Lucky told her.

'I know. How long have you known Walker?'

'About ten years.'

'What is your real name?'

'I'm not at liberty to say.'

'What was your profession?'

'A theological instructor.'

'A priest?'

'I am a *défroqué*.'

'How very interesting. Why were you defrocked?'

'I got married,' he said.

'And now? Where is your wife?'

'That would be telling,' he said.

'I think you are Lucan,' Hildegard said.

'No you don't.'

'Have it your own way. There is every sign that you are the wanted man.'

'My job is just to collect from the aiders and abetters. Lucan is a name in the newspapers. He could be dead.'

'Why does Walker send you to collect?'

'Oh, he sometimes collects himself. But I look more like Lucan.'

She studied his face. 'Yes, in a way you do. In a way you don't. It could be you were once a priest, though. You have a touch of that theological look that can never be thrown off. Only a touch. Now look, Lucky, you are going to deal with one question. You knew Heinrich Esk, that theological student at the Protestant college in Munich, let us say about ten, eleven years ago, didn't you?'

'Twelve years ago,' he said.

'As I've told you, I worked some miracles,' said Hildegard. 'And that is the truth.'

'Undoubtedly. But you were a fraud. A fake stigmatic. Heinrich told me everything. He died of leukaemia, you know.'

'What do you want from me?' Hildegard said.

'Advice. I sold my soul to the Devil, as I've already told you.'

'And you want it back?'

'I want it back.'

'You must break with Walker for a start,' she said.

'That would be difficult.'

'I know. Well, I can't take you both on as patients.'

'I think you have no choice.' Suddenly, Lucky produced a small package. 'I brought you this from Scotland,' he said, passing the little box to Hildegard.

'You thought of me in Scotland,' she said, opening the little parcel with many exclamations of quite genuine appreciation of the crystal pendant.

'I thought of you all the time,' he said.

'That is a normal reaction towards an analyst. And what were you doing in Scotland, exactly?'

'I'm afraid that's a secret. Your other Lucan is furious because I came to you. In fact, I've been round the world in the past twenty-five years. I've been short of money at times and had to be a salesman of textbooks on Presbyterianism and physiotherapy; I've been a gentleman's gentleman – I did well. I've been a genealogist helping the Mormons to trace their ancestry – that was too dangerous, though – I had to make trips to London. What a pity: it was lucrative.'

'And how did you become a priest?'

'Well, I hid in a monastery for a time.'

'That didn't make you a priest.'

'Well, not quite. I just went around with a dog collar.'

'Most of the money wasted on psychoanalysis,' Hildegard said, 'goes on time spent unravelling the lies of the patient. Your time is up.'

'Am I Lucan?' he said. 'I want you to know that I believe in myself.'

8

Maria Twickenham, separated from her husband, attracted many men, but did not greatly encourage them. Maria's reputation was not the subject of scandal or gossip. But the police inspectors who called at her house the day after the murder of Lord Lucan's nanny in November 1974 were not to know that. They were unable to exclude from their minds a possibility that the two were lovers, beautiful as she was, handsome as he was.

It was on the morning of the day after Lord Lucan's disappearance that the police were at Maria's door. One in uniform, two in civilian clothes. There was no answer. They returned in the evening. A man of about forty answered the door.

The uniformed man said, 'Good afternoon. Is Mrs Twickenham at home?'

'She is my wife. She's in South Africa. I am Alfred Twickenham.'

'May we have a word with you, sir?'

'What about?'

'I believe you and your wife are close friends of Lord Lucan. We're wondering about his whereabouts in view of the tragedy that occurred at his home last night.'

'What tragedy?' said Alfred.

'I'd have thought you would have heard,' said the police-man. 'The children's nurse was murdered and the wife severely wounded. The news has been on TV and it's all over the papers. Surely you have heard?'

'Oh, vaguely,' said the man.

'He was a friend of yours. May we come in a minute? We're the Metropolitan Police. We'd like to ask a few questions.'

'Oh, I can't help you. He isn't so very close a friend.' They tramped in while he continued, 'I don't know Lucan all that well.'

In the dining room, where he took them, Alfred didn't invite them to sit down. He stood twirling the atlas-globe: his small daughter did her homework in here. 'My wife,' he said, 'knew Lucan better than me.'

'"*Knew*"?'

'Well, she probably still does know him. Remember, though, Lucky Lucan plays baccarat and we both play bridge predominantly. There's a difference.'

'Suppose,' said one of the plain clothes men, 'that I told you a car that he was using was seen parked in this street at eleven or thereabouts last night?'

'I don't know about that. My wife is in South Africa just now. Perhaps she would know more about Lord Lucan.'

'When did you last see Lord Lucan?'

'I can't remember.'

'Roughly speaking?' said one of the men.

'I can't remember. I see so many people. I think I saw him a month ago at the races.'

'And this is the first time you've heard about the murder and the attack on Lady Lucan in Lower Belgrave Street last night?' The man's eyes were wandering over the polished sideboard, the silver, as if he really wasn't expecting a straight answer.

'But I don't follow murders. I have quite enough to do, as you can imagine. I sell milk.'

'Sell milk?'

'Yes, I run a milk concern.'

'Oh, yes.' One of the other policemen had come to the rescue. 'Twickenham's Dairy Products.'

'That's right,' said Alfred.

'But isn't it upsetting for you to hear about a murder in the house of someone you know? We are looking for Lucan. He's disappeared. How does that affect you?'

'It's devastating. But he plays baccarat and poker, and my wife and I don't. We always played bridge.'

'Thank you, sir, for your cooperation.'

'Don't mention it.'

Alfred felt strongly that his house and office phones were already being tapped. Next morning he stopped at the Army and Navy Stores, where he put through a call. 'Have you heard the news?' he said to the man who answered the phone. 'Well, he's on his way to Caithness. Yes, you know where. Right. I'm calling from a box. If he passes by you . . . Of course, do just that. Oh, poor Lucky!'

At four in the afternoon Alfred went to pick up his daughter from day school.

'I wonder,' said the father, 'if anyone asks you did I have a visitor last night, could you tell them to mind their own business? Just that. Mind their own business.'

'Quite right, Daddy,' said the child.

'No one has the right to ask.'

'I know.'

The child was used to her father's friends' appearances. There was a maintenance and alimony case extending from the far-away mother, and the daughter was quite convinced that her parents had every right and reason to keep their

44

private life private. Her best friends at school, five of them, were in roughly the same position.

'Why did I do it?' Alfred asked himself in his more mature years. 'Why did I cover up his whereabouts? Why? And so many of us did it. Why? The police knew very well we were doing so. There was something about Lucan. I wonder if that's really him they've seen, wherever it is. And why, if so, do his friends feel they must protect him, with all that blood, let's face it, on his hands?'

Blood on his hands. Blood all over his clothes that night of the murder. He did not go straight to Caithness after all, but to some other people in the country, and then to some others, and finally to Caithness, while someone else parked the car he had borrowed in Newhaven.

Maria Twickenham had been beautiful in a way which is not accountable, not to be reckoned by separate features. She was tall and gawky, long-legged, knock-kneed; her nose, too long, went very slightly awry; her mouth, a lovely shape, was definitely too wide; her greyish eyes were nicely spaced but dull and too small; her complexion, perfectly smooth, was, however, drab. How all these factors combined to make her into a striking beauty was inexplicable.

On her return to London to finalise her divorce, Maria heard the story of Lucan's visit from her husband. He felt the young daughter was bound to provide a version of Lucan's visit followed by that of the exciting policemen. At the time Maria accepted Alfred's actions as normal.

And now, decades later, Maria Twickenham read in the paper of yet another sighting of the missing seventh Earl. According to this report he was observed reclining in a hammock, in a British fruit merchant's luxurious garden some-where small and, to Maria, forgettable, in East Africa. He appeared to have been plastically altered but was still, with the help of a computer's identikit system, recognisable. The reporter of this news had returned next day with a photographer but the hounded one, having sensed danger, had gone. At the house nobody could help. 'A white man of about sixty lying in a hammock? You must be mad. People have been turning up here all morning. I'm going to rename my house *Pilgrim's Rest*. Anyway, there's no one here this time of year . . .'

Maria thought back over the years which had done so much to change her life, her personality, her looks, her principles, her everything in a way, little by little. She thought back.

To Maria the memory was like that pill-box veiled hat she had found among her old things, dating from the early 'seventies, last worn at the Derby. She could not wear the hat any more, nor could she again accept her husband's concealment of Lucan. Certainly, she knew that if it were to happen to her, if it were to happen that a Lucan should turn up blood-stained and frantic with a perfectly ridiculous story about passing a basement window and seeing his wife being attacked by a man, Maria, herself, would not clean him up, feed him and pass him on to the next set of good friends. Friendship? Yes, but there can be too severe a strain on friendship. In friendship there is a point of collapse – a murderer revealed, or a traitor – they are people-within-people hitherto unknown.

But what was the difference, Maria wondered, between then and now? More than a quarter of a century was the difference. Alfred had married again, had died. There was something in the air one breathed. Habits change. States of mind change. Collective moods change. The likeable, working-class, murdered young nanny was now the main factor. At the time the centre of the affair was Lucan.

Maria's daughter Lacey, now over thirty, had started in her late teens to influence her mother in a quite natural and unpremeditated way. Having read the most sensible and well-informed of the books on the subject of Lucan, Maria's daughter said, 'How could you ever know such a type? What possessed Daddy to help him to escape? But how could he have been a friend in any case, such a ghastly snob? Anyway, if he could kill once he could kill again, no matter he wasn't tried for murder, the risk of his being a killer is overwhelming. Hadn't anyone any feelings for the poor lovely nurse-girl? Did everyone really believe he could be excused for attempting to kill his wife simply because he didn't like her and didn't want her to have custody of the children? Was Lucan mad?'

In some cases, Lacey reflected, there comes a moment when the best of friends, the most admiring, most affectionate, when faced with a certain person's repeated irrational behaviour, had to admit that the person is more or less mad. 'Mad' covers a whole minefield of mental conditions.

Maria's daughter, now beginning to be free, her children already in their teens, wanted to write a book. People who want to write books do so because they feel it to be the easiest thing they can do. They can read and write, they can afford any of the instruments of book-writing such as pens, paper, computers, tape-recorders, and generally by the time they have reached this decision, they have had a simple education. Lacey's main experience was based on her mother's, which was the fact that she had known the missing, probably the late, Lord Lucan. Lacey took her mother's bundle of press-cuttings, she read all the articles and books about Lucky Lucan that she could lay hands on. Then she started on a series of interviews with some of the living remnants of his life. Not many would consent to see her, and those few who did were mostly convinced that Lucan had committed suicide, either to avoid justice or to avoid injustice, as the case might be. One charming widower, a former acquaintance of the missing Earl as an under-graduate, was more forthcoming. He had retired to a stone house in Perthshire.

'If I had my time again,' he told Lacey, 'I would have looked into the affair with meticulous thoroughness. I would have solved the mystery.'

'Don't you feel that enough was done at the time?' Lacey said.

'I certainly don't. There was a kind of psychological paral-ysis, almost an unconscious conspiracy to let him get away. It was not only that he was a member of the aristocracy, a prominent upper-class fellow, it was that he had pitched his life and all his living arrangements to that proposition. His proposition was: I am a seventh Earl, I am an aristocrat, therefore I can do what I like, I am untouchable. For a few days after the murder, this attitude over-awed the investi-gators and his friends alike. Besides, it was not an ordinary murder, not a shooting affair, it was a horrible bloody slaugh-ter; his wife was in hospital with gaping head wounds which she said were inflicted by him. He was seen by friends with blood on his trousers but they couldn't, or in other words didn't want to, believe he had perpetrated all that violence. In those first days, and even first weeks, he managed to get away. He did so on the sheer strength of his own hypnotic act. A similar case, before your time, was the escape of the traitors Maclean and Burgess. Maclean was particularly upper-class-conscious (although he was nothing, really) but it took everyone in, rooted them to the spot when the facts broke in the Foreign Office. They got away purely on the hypnosis of their life-stylish act.'

Lacey listened intently. Before Dr Joseph Murray, as his name was, had finished his meditative discourse, she had started, with hope in her heart, to form a plan.

'You say if you had your time again . . .' said Lacey.

'Yes, I would have plunged right in. I think I could have nabbed him. The police were slow. The friends who aided and abetted Lucan ran rings around the police. Those police were used to low-life criminals from the streets and from the rooming houses of Mayfair and Soho. Clever sharpsters, they were unnerved by the stonewalling toffs; they were not exactly abject, not at all. But they were hesitant, out of their depth. When one of the friends of Lucan exclaimed when approached, "Oh dear, and good nannies are so scarce!" the police took this for heartless reality instead of a quip in poor taste. That sort of thing. I would have known how to deal with the situation the very night of the murder. I wouldn't, believe me, Lacey, have been overwhelmed.'

'It's not too late,' said Lacey.

'What?'

'Hopefully, you could still find him,' said Lacey with the utmost enthusiasm. 'I want to interview him, only. I wouldn't want necessarily to hand him over. I think he must be alive.'

'Perhaps. Personally, I believe in justice, but . . .'

'How could there be justice in such a case?' said Lacey.

Joseph Murray smiled at her. 'You're quite right, of course. Human justice could never equal the crime. All the books and articles – such piles of them – that have been written on the subject, appear to agree that Lucan, if guilty, was very guilty. Indeed I incline to agree with the theory – you'll find it in Marnham's book – that there was an accomplice, a hit-man. If so, that hit-man is somewhere on the loose. I must say that the theory is highly tenable. If

49

sound, it would explain a number of loose factors, small as that number is.'

'Will you help me to launch a new search?'

'Oh, no. Not now.'

'Oh, yes. *Now*, Dr Murray,' said pretty Lacey. 'Now,' she repeated.

'Call me Joe,' he said.

'Joe,' she said, 'now,' she said.

Joe was the youngest son of a prosperous family. He was now in his sixties, not too tall, fairly slim. He had never married again after his young wife had died while he was teaching at Cambridge. He was a virtual and ardent zoologist and in fact took up a zoologist's interest in many human affairs outside of his personal life. About Lucan he appeared to feel as he spoke, almost zoologically. What species was Lucan? Joe was all the more curious on this score, in that he had been a friend of Lucan's. How he regretted not having had long conversations with Lucan outside of topics such as baccarat, craps, poker, *vingt-et-un*, and the possible winner of the three-thirty. Now that he came to think of it, he had never really thought of Lucan, so that when the scandal broke and Lucan did not step forward to clear himself it did seem to Joe as if Lucan could possibly be, in a way hitherto partly concealed from his acquaintances, bad-tempered to a degree that was outside of human, and was something else. Well, he reflected, that's perhaps another way of saying that poor Lucan was mad. Lucan besides was a silk purse, and it was useless to expect such an object to turn into something so good, so true, as a sow's ear.

'You know,' Joe said then to Lacey, 'I think there must have been an accomplice, a hit-man.'

'Why do you think so?'

'I knew Lucan. Not closely, but enough. When we were undergraduates. He had no imagination, or at least very little. Now, think of what he claimed in his letters and statements to his friends and on the phone to his mother the night of the murder. He said he was passing the house in Lower Belgrave Street where his wife and children were staying, when he saw from the pavement a man in the basement attacking his wife, and went to the rescue, and got all bloodied. It is the question of his seeing a man. To someone of limited imagination it would be a natural excuse – *a man*. The man was most probably, in fact, the man prominent in his mind and memory, the hit-man, the accomplice.'

'The police network failed,' said Lacey, 'to produce any man on the run that night. They found no accomplice. There was no light in the basement, and nothing could be seen, from the street, anyway.'

'The police didn't find Lucan, either. They were slow throughout. If you'd like to leave your notes with me, and any cuttings that are contemporaneous with the crime, I'll give a bit of thought to the subject. Now, my dear, you'll stay for a bite, won't you? My helper puts it ready in the microwave, and there's always more than enough for two.'

Lacey accepted the invitation and made herself at home at the kitchen table. She told Joe how she was separated from her husband, awaiting a divorce; there was no real fault on either side but that was how it was. Joe told her she was good-looking, perhaps even prettier than her mother had been at her age. He remembered Maria Twickenham quite well, she had been around and knew Lucan, 'though not intimately'. But who had known Lucan intimately?

'Lucan – who knew him really?' Joe said.

'His wife? His parents?'

'Only partially – none of them could have known him, fully.'

'He talked previous to the murder about murdering his wife.'

'Yes, well, talk . . . People often talk that way. It doesn't mean anything, necessarily; in fact, quite the opposite. It could be argued that if he intended the murder he wouldn't have talked about it.'

'I want you to come with me and see that priest I mentioned in my letter. Is he still at the same parish?'

'Father Ambrose? I got a Christmas card. Yes.'

'You'll come with me?'

'I don't know about that. And there's Benny Rolfe.'

'Who's he?'

Benny Rolfe, Joe explained, was a prosperous business-man who was once a friend of Lucan's. It was rumoured that he financed Lucan's sojourn abroad. 'You must remember that if Lucan's alive, he may have changed more radically in appearance than the mere passage of years can explain. He would have undergone perhaps extensive plastic surgery.'

'Then how would his friends recognise him?'

'That's the point. They would expect to not quite recognise him immediately; they would expect him to have undergone facial surgery. Which leaves the way wide open for a crook, posing as Lucan, making an understandably rapid visit to a friend, to pass a few general remarks, collect his money and run. Lucan could be dead while the conspiracies to elude the law continue. All I want to say, really, my dear, is that your search for the real Lucan might be fruitless.'

'Could he get away with it?'

'Enough,' said Joe, 'has been written about Lucan to prompt even an amateur actor of feeble intelligence. He would be in a position to know practically every detail of the past. A fake Lucan might be entirely convincing.'

'Obviously,' said Lacey, 'you think Lucan's dead.'

'I think nothing. I think nothing at all on the subject. His friends are divided fifty–fifty on the possibility that he killed himself soon after the murder. I should say fifty–fifty.'

'Would you know if you met him –'

'If he was real or fake? Yes, I think I should. Perhaps . . .'

'Then let's find him,' said Lacey, with so much of the enthusiasm of the novice that Joe was lost for words; he simply smiled. 'Am I talking a lot of nonsense?' she said.

'Yes and no. I must say that without trying, nobody gets anything, anywhere. And then, of course, the whole Lucan story is thoroughly surrealistic. The only real things about it are a girl's battered body in a mailsack, his wife's head wounds, her testimony that she had been attacked by him, and blood all over the place. Apart from those vital factors – and they are vital, to say the least, aren't they? – the disappearance of Lucan partakes of the realistic-surrealistic. He was ready to disappear to avoid bankruptcy; on the other hand his friends were numerous. They seem to have been faithful in the class-conscious sense. I find very little evidence that any of the friends, the aiders and abetters as they might be, cared a damn for Lucan the man.'

'Mummy found him quite amusing,' said Lacey. 'But do you know, she told me that if she had that time over again she wouldn't like Daddy's covering up for Lucan. Something has happened to her conscience between then and now. Has this happened to other people who were involved at the time?'

'Oh, quite likely. We are not the same people as we were a quarter of a century ago. We are necessarily different in our ideas. In my view it is an economic phenomenon. We cannot afford to be snobs. Since Lucan's day, snobs have been greatly marginalised. Not entirely. Benny Rolfe, who is reputed to be Lucan's benefactor, is an old-fashioned snob. Few people today would take Lucan and his pretensions seriously, as they rather tended to do in the 'seventies. I daresay even Benny Rolfe is tiring of Lucan, if he's still alive.'

9

On the road to Caithness Joe and Lacey respectively marvelled how they seemed to have 'known each other all our lives'.

'You make me feel young again,' he said.

She liked the sound of that. She was hardly expecting to track down the elusive, the perhaps non-existent Earl; not really. It was the prospect of a chase that excited her, this promising and enjoyable beginning. They were on their way, now, to a house they had merely heard of, right in the far north of Scotland. It was assumed that Benny Rolfe, whose house it was, would very likely be away. He was in any case hardly ever there. It would be all the more convenient perhaps to question the housekeeper and the houseman who Joe knew lived there in perpetuity. If someone like Lucan had been to see Benny, those people would know. Of course they wouldn't talk. Not really talk. But there were ways of talking and talking, and something somehow might trickle through. 'Of course we mustn't ask direct questions,' said Joe.

'Oh, it would be fatal, I agree.'

The great lovely steep hills were all around them. The feeling of northern nature, a whole geography minding very much its own business, cautious, alien, cold and haughty, began here. The sky rolled darkly amid patches of white light. On they drove, north, north.

*

Yes, there was a light high up there in the turret. The bell, which was an old-fashioned pull-bell which pealed hysterically throughout the house, brought no response for the first ten minutes of their wait in the drive, in the dark.

Joe fetched a torch from his car and started prowling around, while Lacey stood hugging her coat around her, staring up at the light in the Gothic tower. Suddenly she heard a shuffle, and in a moment the door opened to a flood of light.

Joe reappeared very quickly.

'Yes?' said a man's voice.

'This is the residence of Mr Benny Rolfe, isn't it?'

'This is Adanbrae Keep. It was you that rang up?' the speaker said. He was a middle-aged, red-haired and bearded man wearing a handyman's apron. 'I thought you'd come early, gave you up. Well, you know Benny isn't here. Come in, if you will. Come in and sit yourselves down.'

The hall of Adanbrae Keep was welcoming enough, with new-looking chintzes. The man put a click-light to the fire which started to blaze up obediently.

'Benny's in France,' he said. 'Sit yourselves down. Would you like a cup of tea? My name's Gordon.'

'Yes,' said Joe.

'Oh, please,' said Lacey.

'Are you all alone here?' said Joe.

'No, no. There's the stable man, Pat Reilly, there's my garden boy, Jimmie – he's gone off to lend a hand at the golf tavern and make himself a bit extra, there's Mrs Kerr, she is in her room, but she won't be in bed yet, if you'd like to meet her I could get her. I'll just put on the kettle.'

'I'd like to see Mrs Kerr,' said Lacey when he had left the hall.

Joe said, 'We've no right to trouble them. Benny wouldn't like it. He'd think us awfully rude. It's all right just to call in, but we mustn't seem to snoop, or probe, or anything like that.'

'I'd like to probe,' said Lacey.

Just then, down the main staircase came a short dark woman of about forty with a wide lipsticked smile. 'I'm Betty Kerr,' she said. 'I heard you arrive. We just about gave you up. Are you staying anywhere around here?'

She had a pink roller, probably overlooked, still in her hair. She sat down on one of the chintz chairs. Joe told her the hotel they had booked for the night, of which she expressed approval.

'We thought we would just look in,' said Lacey, 'as Mr Rolfe isn't available, we tried everywhere, but we only wanted to sort of trace someone who might have been here recently. An old friend of Dr Murray's – that's my companion here – that we want to get in touch with.'

'What name?' said Betty Kerr.

In came Gordon the Red bearing a tray of tea-cups with the pot and jug.

'Lucan,' said Joe.

'No, I don't know of a Lucan,' said Betty Kerr. She poured out the tea and handed it out to the couple. This was an event, plainly, and she liked it. 'Did he play golf? There was a gentleman here playing golf. But no, he wasn't a Lucan. A wee man with a bag of old clubs like forty years ago. Gordon had to clean his mashie with emery paper.'

'No, the old university friend I'm trying to contact is tall.'

Gordon was hovering around. 'That could be the gentleman who was to dinner about three weeks ago. He spent the night here. He was "John" to Benny, I seem to remember. Just a minute, I'll look at the book.'

The visitors' book on its lectern stood near a closed door which led to the drawing-room. Joe went over to it with

Gordon, and they looked at the open page. 'Nobody here; he didn't sign at all, the man I'm thinking of,' said Gordon. 'There's very few visitors, so it would be on this page.'

Joe, by way of curiosity, turned back a few pages, but although he recognised a few of the names, nothing corresponding to Lucan was there. 'Anyway, Lucan's second name was John and generally applied to him when he was a student. It means nothing, though, John by itself could be anybody.'

'A tall man with white hair, in his sixties, squarish face,' said Gordon helpfully. 'In good form, I would say. I didn't take much notice.'

They had returned to the fireplace. Joe realised that the description would fit Lucan as he might be today.

It was plain to both Joe and Lacey that they had probed enough. They had neither of them desired to go blatantly behind Benny's back. Joe had already told Lacey he intended to drop Benny a line explaining his search for Lucan. 'After all, it's a legitimate search,' he had remarked to Lacey.

Now he said, 'Well, thank you, Gordon, and you, too, Mrs Kerr.'

'I hope,' said Lacey, 'we haven't disturbed you.'

'Mind how you go. Take your time,' said Betty Kerr. 'You could have stayed for a meal, but we don't have much in the house. Not like when that gentleman was here. Smoked salmon and lamb cutlets two days running.'

'Smoked salmon and lamb chops . . .'

'That's right. Benny ordered them specially for him. His preference.'

Next morning on their way still further north Joe was truly optimistic. They had already celebrated the final words of the Adanbrae Keep domestics, but Joe could not keep off the subject. It was like winning a bet at long odds.

'"Smoked salmon and lamb chops served two meals running . . ." Benny knows Lucan's preferences. What a fool Lucan is to allow himself to be trapped by that characteristic of his; that eccentric taste for smoked salmon and cutlets day in, day out for years on end. It had to be Lucan.'

'Or someone like him, who has studied his ways from the press accounts,' said astute Lacey. 'And Benny Rolfe would expect him to have had his face fixed.'

The landscape was bleak and flat, below a pearly sky. They seemed to be driving into the sky. St Columba's monastery, lately established, was some way out of a silent, almost deserted but well-kept stone village.

A young bespectacled lay brother bade them wait a minute. Joe had telephoned in advance. Sure enough, Father Ambrose appeared as if by magic with his black habit floating wide around him. You could not see if he was thin or fat. He had the shape of a billowing pyramid with his small white-haired head at the apex as if some enemy had hoisted it there as a trophy of war. From under his habit protruded an enormous pair of dark-blue track shoes on which he lumbered towards them. As he careered along the cold cloister he read what was evidently his Office of the day; his lips moved; plainly, he didn't believe in wasting time and did believe in letting the world know it. When he came abreast of Lacey and Joe he snapped shut his book and beamed at them.

'Joe,' he said.

'Ambrose, how are you? And how goes it in your new abode? This is Lacey, daughter of Maria Twickenham. Remember Maria?'

'Well, well. How do you do? How's Maria?'

They followed him into a polished parlour; it smelt keenly of cleanliness.

It will be seen that the above description of Ambrose applies to a man very convinced of himself. Calling or no calling, Ambrose had arranged his life so that there was no challenge, no fear of any but the most shallow pitfalls. He could hardly err, there was no scope for it. He was good at raising funds.

'You want to know about Lucan,' said Ambrose.

'Yes, we're looking for him.'

'People have been looking for him this quarter-century. I brought down the press-cuttings for you. I'll have to go shortly but you can stay and look through them.' He had lumbered over to an open glass-fronted cabinet and now placed a very thick package on the table before them. In the meantime the young lay brother came in with a tray of milky coffee with dry sweet biscuits. He placed them on the table and withdrew, almost disintegrated, so shadowy was he.

Exactly above the parlour where Joe and Lacey set about their perusal of the press-cuttings was a bedroom, a simple monk's cell, eight by seven feet with a mullioned window open to the vast northern plain in which St Columba's monastery had been put up, not very long ago.

There was a tap on the door and without waiting for a reply the tapper, Ambrose, floated silently in. His finger was laid on his lips.

'Say nothing,' said Ambrose. 'Make no sound. Lucan, you have to go.'

'Why, what's wrong?'

'Lower your voice. A couple of people are intensely looking for you. I say intensely. They're here in the monastery, in the parlour just underneath.'

'Here? Oh, my God, have they got a warrant?'

'They're not the police, Lucan, they are worse. They are Joe Murray with the daughter of, guess who? – Maria Twickenham. Her name's Lacey. Yes, Maria's daughter and the image of her mother. They have apparently nothing to do but hunt you down. Lacey is writing a book about you, of course.'

'Maria's daughter. Oh, my God.'

Ambrose placed his finger once more to his lips. 'Silence is your only hope.' He explained that he was keeping the couple occupied with a large file of press-cuttings.

'About me?'

'Of course about you. I don't want them to suspect anything. I gave them my whole collection to look at.'

'That will help them, Ambrose.'

'Meantime, though, you can be on your way.'

'Where to?'

'Keep to the east, Lucan, and I'll direct them south-west somehow. You'll find a bed-and-breakfast at Kirkwall. They'll never think of tracing you to that little hole.'

Some twenty minutes later the lay brother was observed by Lacey escorting a black-robed monk with a bulging hold-all to a light-coloured station-wagon. They shook hands and the car departed. Lacey looked back at her copy of the London paper which held a not-very-revealing article about Lucan. She said, suddenly, 'You know, this would be a good place for Lucan to hide. Are you getting anything out of these cuttings? I'm not, I seem to have seen them all.'

'They're fairly new to me,' said Joe. 'I wouldn't mind another half-hour's go at them, if that's all right by you, Lacey, dear.'

'Yes of course it's all right.' She felt how strongly he was attracted by her, and began to consider to herself that the

61

idea of a love affair between them might not be a bad idea, even if it was only an idea.

The door opened and in wafted Ambrose.

'How are you getting on?' He fingered one of the press-cutting piles. 'How strange it must be,' he said, 'to be Lucan, if he is still alive. From what I knew of him his thoughts will be entirely on evading capture, all the time; every day, every move, every contact with the world, all his acquaintances – all, all, revolving around that one proposition, that he must avoid capture.'

'He must be haunted by what he did,' said Lacey.

'Not him,' said Joe.

Ambrose joined in with a conviction that almost betrayed him. 'Oh no, he doesn't think of the murder,' he said. 'Wherever he is, whoever he is now, he thinks of nothing but escape.'

'Do you see him ever?' said Joe.

'Not for sure. He has pretenders.'

'Not much of a cause to pretend to,' said Lacey.

'Now, what . . .' said Ambrose. He seated himself as comfortably as he could at the central table, which was at present covered with newspaper pages and cuttings. 'What, Lacey, brings you to this manhunt?'

'I'm going to write a book.'

'And you think you'll find him where everyone else has failed? – the journalists, the police and others – who knows? There have been sightings, no findings, for a quarter-century.'

'What a fascinating subject it is,' said Joe. 'I want to help Lacey all I can.'

'Would you tip off the police if you found him?' said Ambrose.

'Yes,' said Lacey. 'No,' said Joe, simultaneously.

They laughed. 'I think he must have had a lot of hardships,' Joe said. 'He made a blunder.'

'Oh, but he fully intended to kill his wife,' said Lacey. 'The intention was there. Which one he killed is basically irrelevant. He had been talking about murdering his wife.'

'People talk, they talk,' said Ambrose. 'It was a dreadful, frightful affair, there's no doubt about that.'

'Why is it,' said Lacey, 'that most people – those who didn't know him as well as his friends and acquaintances – didn't at all believe he would take his own life? He was driving round the very night of the murder seeing friends of his and phoning his mother, and he also wrote some letters to his friends. Instructions about his overdrafts, garbled explanations, a declaration that he was going to lie low, but no good-byes, no hint that he might end his life, and no remorse, not a word of sorrow about the death of young Sandra, poor young Sandra. Yes, if I located him tomorrow I would tip off the police.'

'And you, Ambrose?' said Joe.

'Oh, in my trade you know how it is,' said the priest, and left it at that.

They were on their way south, gladly leaving behind them the flatlands of the north, the pearl-grey skies full of watery foreboding and squawking seafowl.

Lacey had with her a pile of press-cuttings – there would be about thirty – which Ambrose had arranged to be photocopied for her. He had been anxious to get rid of the couple, had not even offered to show them round the fairly new monastery.

'The man we are looking for is stupid but cunning, not clever,' she said.

'That's very true. One would think you'd known him, Lacey, as I did. He was stupid and boring. You had to draw him out. Sometimes, if you succeeded in drawing him out, he could be quite amusing though.'

'But not clever.'

'Oh no, not clever. He had a flair for gambling. Always lost in the end but he had a physical presence, so that a gaming house would find him an asset, egging on the novices and so on.'

'Are you sure you'd recognise him?' said Lacey.

'No. I don't think I would. At least, not face-on because I'd bet that he's had facial surgery. But you know, I might recognise him from the back. His shape, his movements, the way he walked. Now, if you find him, what are you going to do?'

'Arrange an interview.'

'He'd never agree to that.'

'Perhaps he would have to agree,' said Lacey. 'Or face exposure.'

Joe did not reply. Plainly, he thought, she has it both romantically and practically worked out. Why doesn't she just write the book? A book about Lucan. Why bother with Lucan himself?

Lacey went on, 'You see, I'll do a deal with him.'

'I was under the impression,' said Joe, 'that you wanted to get him arrested and tried.'

'In a way,' she said. 'Because I think he is guilty.'

'Oh, you could never be sure. As I remember him he was an unpredictable fellow. Although I didn't care for him much to begin with, well, as I say, he rather grew on me.'

They were silent for a good while. Then suddenly Lacey said, 'Oh my God!'

'What's the matter?' He was driving, and slowed down.

'Did you see from the window that monk getting into a station-wagon? He was saying goodbye to that lay brother. Then he drove off.'

'Yes, I did look out just then. I saw you were looking.'

'That couldn't be Lucan, could it?'

Joe thought for a moment. 'I only saw him from the back. It could have been Lucan, yes. From the height it could have been. But so could anyone that height and, I suppose, age, look like Lucan.'

'Wouldn't it have been natural for him to have come straight to Ambrose from Benny Rolfe's? He left early from Adanbrae Keep. Wouldn't he have come straight on to Ambrose, his old gambling friend?'

'Very likely,' said Joe. 'And now I come to think of it, that man could have been Lucan.'

'We shouldn't jump to conclusions,' she said. 'Be cautious, Joe. Dozens of men, from the back, could be Lucan.'

'It was a station-wagon,' he said, in a stunned way.

'Was it a Ford?' she said.

'Well, of course I don't know. It might have been a Ford but I couldn't swear.'

'Nor could I.'

'He could have stopped over at St Columba's. Almost certainly he would do that.'

'But Father Ambrose didn't know his whereabouts,' said Lacey.

'Ambrose is a liar. Always very shifty. All obsessed gamblers are liars.'

'The Prior of a monastery?'

'I think it possible,' said Joe, 'for a man to be a holy person and a glib liar at the same time. He might be trying to protect a man.'

They were now well into Easter Ross. Traffic began to appear as if out of the scenery, and they pulled up at a small lakeside hotel called The Potted Heid.

The Lucan who had been seen off at St Columba's by the lay brother was the one called Lucky. Having been directed east, he decided to go south. If Joe Murray and Maria Twickenham's daughter were tracking him he wanted to keep an eye on them.

To the south, to the south. Lucky Lucan was heading for the airport.

But he was not at all sure how far he could trust Ambrose. Had he put the couple on his trail? Had they recognised him while he hurried across the courtyard to the hired station-wagon, so wretchedly noticeable? The couple had been in the parlour engrossed, Ambrose had said, in newspaper cuttings. They were writing a book about him. Why did Ambrose keep newspaper cuttings about the Lucan case? Benny Rolfe, mused Lucan, was inconsiderate, was scared. He should have arranged the money payments by transfer instead of forcing him to come and collect in this eccentric way. But Benny was scared of being caught as an accomplice. No guts. Lucan decided to find a road-house somewhere near Inverness. They would probably have to pass that way. He would wait the next morning, get another car, and if possible, follow them.

As it fell out, Joe and Lacey delayed their departure from The Potted Heid to make love. It was after ten in the morning that they dumped their bags downstairs, and looked into the breakfast room. The high-priced and unjovial hotel produced some inscrutable coffee. Breakfast was definitely over. On the table where they were served the coffee which slopped over the saucer was a half-filled ashtray. Lacey, in great high spirits, pointed this out to the sullen houseman who totally ignored her. They went to pay the bill and were told that Joe's credit card didn't work. Then Lacey's didn't work. Joe said, 'Let's see,' and adjusted the card machine on a workable flat surface. His card then worked. They felt good to be on their way. They felt very good, anyway, at the grand beginning of a love affair, free and full of enterprise, without any mess of impediments.

The hills, glens, lochs, wrapped themselves around the lovers' mood. The weather was good, with alternating cloud and sun-breaks, making spectacular effects.

They stopped beyond Inverness for lunch at a good pub, Muir's Cairn, this time a lucky find. Could Lucan have gone ahead of them? About ten cars were parked outside the pub, two of them white, a medium-sized Renault and a family Ford. Inside, it was warm, there was a good crowd of people at the tables and at the bar. They were given a table by the window with a fine view.

'Now,' said Lacey, 'let's look at the clients.' Joe was already looking over the top of the menu.

There was no sign of a single man vaguely resembling the monk who had been seen into the station-wagon. From where they sat it was difficult to see everyone around the bar which stretched away into a more public salon.

Lacey glanced out of the window behind her. It was raining, now. Two or three people and a couple were making towards their cars. One man in particular drew her attention. He was putting on a dark-green waterproof short jacket, and got into a white car. He was not the man they were looking for but it now occurred to Lacey that it was quite possible the suspect Lucan had changed cars. It would be possible to do so between Caithness and Inverness, and certainly not difficult for a man of Lucan's resources. She remarked on this to Joe. He, in turn, observed that the further south they went the less likely were they to find their man.

'And besides, he might have gone directly south after leaving Benny's place,' said Joe.

'But you know Betty Kerr said he was going north. That might mean the monastery. He was very close to Ambrose in his younger days, according to my mother,' Lacey said.

Smoked salmon was on the menu and so were lamb cutlets. Joe pointed this out. 'Sounds delicious,' said Lacey. 'That's my choice.' Around them people at the other tables were being served mainly fish and chips or large salads piled with eatables covered with mayonnaise.

Joe, too, chose smoked salmon followed by lamb cutlets, mainly out of love for Lacey. He was in fact so taken with this charming young woman now in his life that he didn't care very much what he ate. He didn't care very much about finding Lucan, except to make Lacey happy.

In the quite authentic glow of their new love affair they did not focus their full attention on the comings and goings of the other customers. However, when they were served their second course of cutlets with green peas, Joe said to the waitress, 'Is the smoked salmon followed by lamb in great demand today?'

'Oh, yes,' she said, 'it's always a good combine.'

Driving south, maddeningly slow on the road, was a white Ford, quite unusual enough a car in those parts. It was driven by a whitish-haired man who, from behind, might have been their man. They were aware that the amusement of guessing the possibilities of tracing Lucan rather outweighed the possibilities themselves. There were many alternative routes to the south of Caithness. But it was definitely fun. The new lovers were in the mood for fun. Still, the car driving so slowly (why slowly?) in front of them was an exciting fact. The driver wanted them to pass, and in spite of numerous bends and dips that made passing inadvisable, they could sometimes have done so. But Lacey, who was at the wheel that afternoon, didn't do so. She kept doggedly behind the white Ford which kept doggedly at its almost funereal pace, much to the fury of the traffic behind them, which passed both cars as best it could.

'Whoever's in that Ford knows we're positively following him,' said Lacey.

They were approaching a tall wall surrounding a large house. Ahead were a number of people dressed in their best clothes for a wedding. The Ford slowed down even more. It glided towards the huge gates with heraldic designs picked out in gold surmounted by a pair of legendary creatures in stone. The white car caused a few young giggling men and women to make way for it as it swung into the drive. As Joe and Lacey passed they could see on the lawn in front of the house a huge marquee. Loud voices and soft music completed the scene of the wedding. Joe and Lacey drove on.

The tall, white-haired stranger made his way over the lawn to the thronging mass of joyful guests, the men in their formal clothes, and occasionally kilts, the women in their smart outfits with big black hats, at least five hundred people. At the far end of the marquee the bride and groom could be seen with their young friends, doubled up with laughter. A quintet was playing softly, to suit the two main generations represented. By instinct, the stranger noticed a tall, dove-grey-clad woman and her equally tall and greyly distinguished husband standing apart. He went over to them. 'How do you do? Congratulations. I'm Walker,' he said. 'I'm afraid I hadn't time to change but they knew I wouldn't. Glad to be here, anyway.' Having said this and shaken hands with the couple, he helped himself to a glass of champagne from a tray that was wafted before him.

'Oh, don't worry about your clothes,' the woman said nervously. The stranger looked down on his dark-grey suit and then beamed up at them. 'So glad you could come, Mr Walker. I don't know half my new son-in-law's friends, I'm afraid.'

'Hundreds of them,' said her husband. 'And hundreds we hardly know on my daughter's side.'

'Well, I'll go and say a word to the happy couple,' said the stranger.

It would have been difficult for him to reach the couple even if he had wanted to. The marquee was very warm both from human heat and from the side-stoves carefully placed along the edges of the tent. The stranger found a spot to stand, and before long was approached by a good-looking middle-aged woman. 'I'm sure we've met somewhere, but I can't place you.'

'Walker,' he said.

'Walker? I don't recall.' She spoke with a strong Scottish accent. 'But I know your face. I'm Bessie Lang.'

'Bessie!' he said. 'Of course. How the years fly!' He took another glass of champagne. She refused one. 'I must remind Bobbie,' said the stranger, 'to give me the guest list. So many people I know here. But of course, the young people, especially on her side, are more or less unknown to me. Oh, there's Bobbie over there' – the stranger waved to the other side of the tent – 'Excuse me, won't you? I have to make myself useful over there. Let's keep in touch.' Then he was gone, lost in another crowd, mingling, smiling, exchanging pleasantries. He shook hands finally with the bridegroom's mother and kilted, lace-shirted father, who were as short, it seemed, as the bride's parents were tall; then, having judged that a good forty minutes had passed, he made his way through the chattering concentration of the Scottish privileged, back to his white Ford.

True enough, on the road, his pursuers had disappeared. Maria Twickenham's daughter and Joe Murray, the latter's name only dimly remembered by Lucan, both of them on the hunt for him. He remembered Maria Twickenham well and felt a great nostalgia for her. If it had been Maria, he might even have revealed himself for twenty minutes. But the daughter . . . And Joe . . . Oh, no, you don't write any book about me, you don't. Ambrose had suspected they were having an affair. 'I know by the way they look over each other's shoulders while they're perusing the press-cuttings,' Ambrose had said. 'There's something about lovers and their slop, I always know it.'

And the girl's name is Lacey, thought Lucan. Very ridiculous. Imagine if I were to put in twelve to fifteen years in a prison cell just to satisfy a girl called Lacey . . .

Anyway he had thrown them at the wedding. Any subsequent enquiries would result in a man called Walker having put in an appearance at the invitation of a man whose name no one remembered.

10

Hildegard had come from Paris by train through the tunnel. She had brought two bulging zip-bags full of documents, a small suitcase, her handbag-briefcase, and what she stood up in. She got a taxi and went to the Manderville Hotel at Queen's Gate, where she had booked a room. In the taxi she put her watch one hour back. It would be one-fifteen in Paris, it was twelve-fifteen here. In Paris Jean-Pierre would be on the phone trying vainly, as he had tried for the past half-hour, to reach her and arrange, as usual, where they would eat lunch. This was the first of the hard and difficult aspects of what Hildegard had set out to do. That was, to disappear without trace. She had in fact decided on this course without fully realising it herself, from the day, the hour, the moment she realised that the Lucan claimants knew about her past.

Jean-Pierre would go round to her office. Ring the bell. No reply. Her secretary – Jean-Pierre would ring her up at home, he would go down to the bar and ring her up. But perhaps no – did Jean-Pierre know her secretary's surname? No, he wouldn't. At three-thirty a young patient beset with unnecessary fears was due to arrive for a session. Dominique, the secretary-receptionist, would by now have let herself in, and would be puzzled by Hildegard's non-arrival. 'Will you take a seat? Dr Wolf will be here any minute,' she would say to the girl. In the meantime, four o'clock having struck, she would ring Jean-Pierre's flat in vain, and then the workshop. 'M. Roget? This is Dominique, Dr Wolf's receptionist. No, there is no sign of Dr Wolf. A patient is waiting. Perhaps you should – yes, please come here. Something must have happened. Please come at once.'

They would ring the hospitals, possibly the police stations. Jean-Pierre would send the patient away with his polite apologies. Eventually, perhaps tomorrow, he might make a statement to the police. Dr Wolf is missing. The police would search her office, the flat she shared with Jean-Pierre. He would be interrogated closely. 'When did you last see Mme Wolf? What was her state of mind?'

He would probably guess her state of mind. He would of course not elaborate on this to the police. He would know she had gone into hiding.

He would wait for a message. About that, she would have to decide. On no account must anyone trace her whereabouts. She had disappeared, perhaps for ever. The Lucans would disappear too, go back to where they had come from; Hildegard thought of them as 'The Lucans', without a thought that only one of them was probably real, and the other a fake.

In Paris, the course of events that Hildegard had imagined more or less took place, except that Jean-Pierre did not report her disappearance to the police.

She had paid up the rent on her office and given notice. She had left the office furniture, but taken her laptop computer and many of the current files, including the Lucan papers. Dominique checked through, wearing her coat and wool cap, ready to go off into her own life, while Jean-Pierre watched. Dominique looked at all the files that were left. 'From my memory,' she said, 'and from my appointments book, the files here belong only to patients who had finished their course. The current files are gone.'

'Who were the current clients?'

'Well, there was Walker, there was Lucky Lucan. There was Mrs Maisie Round, Karl K. Jacobs, and just a minute . . .' She consulted her diary: 'There was Dr Oscar Hertz. Dr Wolf did like Dr Hertz so very much. There was Ruth Ciampino. Mrs William Hane-Busby, also.'

'No French clients?'

'At the moment, none.'

Jean-Pierre was struck by a stab of jealousy. 'Who was Dr Hertz?'

'Dr Oscar Hertz is a recent widower. He has problems of grief and so on.'

'Do you know the addresses and telephone numbers of all the clients whose files are missing?'

She sat down in her coat and typed, with the aid of her appointments book, what little she knew about the list of names she had just given. 'Dr Wolf spoke seldom about her clients. She was friendly, talkative, very nice to me, but she didn't say much about the patients who came to consult her. Now, I'll leave you my office keys. This is the front door. These are the office door – there are two safety-locks.'

'I know,' he said. 'I have copies of the keys.'

'And the keys to the filing cabinet. The keys to Dr Wolf's desk.'

'I don't have those. Leave them with me.'

'Do you want me to make a statement to the police, M. Roget?'

'There's no need to tell the police.'

'Would it not be correct?'

'There is no need.'

'No?'

'No.'

'Suppose,' she said, 'that Dr Wolf has met with an accident?'

'I don't suppose. You do not take half your office archives with you to have an accident.'

Dominique left, a small figure, wrapped in her coat and scarf, her woolly cap, her pay-cheque in her bag, provided by Jean-Pierre, her blonde hair half-covering her pink cheeks.

She closed the door behind her, but immediately he opened it to call her back.

'Leave me your telephone number and your address.'

'It's in my file,' said Dominique, 'but I'm not sure how long I'll be staying in Paris.'

'No?'

'No.'

He asked her, 'Are you in touch with Dr Wolf?'

'Why should I be in touch with Dr Wolf?'

'I mean no offence, Dominique. But if she gets in touch with you, will you let me know?'

'Yes, I will do that, M. Roget. I will certainly tell you.'

Hildegard had long felt that sentimentality was a luxury she could not afford. Perhaps she had always felt it, right back to the time when the family had a pig farm, and the little pigs squealed pitifully, and bled. These things had to be.

She had fourteen brothers and sisters, some old enough to be her mother or father. Someone washed and dressed her, took her to school, fed her: a brother, a mother, a sister, a father, whosoever. She grew up on the pig farm. The sisters and brothers eventually married and went to live each in a house not far away. They continued in the pig business. Hildegard (then Beate) grew up, with all of them around, among the pigs. She went to school, was clever. She fought herself free from her home. She found Heinrich. She made blood-money.

And now she was supposed to ask herself about her loyalty and love for Jean-Pierre in Paris. She knew very well he would be frantically looking for her. She couldn't afford such sweetness. He would expect some sign of her affection. It was too much to ask. And yet the question asked itself. Oh, Jean-Pierre, what else, what else could I have done?

II

Jean-Pierre had packed a small bag and set it aside. He was ready to leave Paris any time, at a moment's notice. Hildegard had been missing over a week and no message from her had reached him. He was more worried by this fact than by her absence, for he was convinced that she was safely settled somewhere of her own choice. She had left her car in the garage, paid up three months in advance. The garage owner could give no explanation, no clue. Jean-Pierre was not anxious for her safety. He brooded only over the fact that she hadn't rung him at his business number or on his mobile telephone.

He made a decision to find her and follow. He began with the list of her patients that Dominique had given him. Only Lucan and Walker had no phone numbers against their names.

'Mrs Maisie Round?' Jean-Pierre spoke in English, and quite well.

'Yes, speaking. Who is it?'

'Jean-Pierre Roget. I am a friend of Dr Hildegard Wolf. I –'

'Where is Dr Wolf? It is shameful that she has left in the middle of my treatment. Her secretary just rang and told me she had left Paris, that was all.'

'I was wondering if you had any clue where she was, Madame.'

The woman started to speak again, shrieking, and did not leave off shrieks until she had come to the point in her discourse where Jean-Pierre broke her off. She shrieked:

'It is nothing short of criminal to leave a patient hamstrung in a sitting in the middle of a course just as I was getting to the heart of the matter and she knew that I was arriving at that point of no return so I am now in deep shock and my psyche is severely damaged and at the end of the day the bottom line is I am going to have my attorney issue a writ against Hildegard Wolf and also have her definitely struck off because it looks like here in Paris she was never registered at all with any school or any institute of psychiatry but I paid her over a period of eight months only to find myself neither divorcing from him nor engaging with Thomas and I am in a preposterous dilemma that she should have spared me as it was her responsibility to address the problem right from . . .'

At this point Jean-Pierre quietly hung up. He fixed himself a vodka-tonic and rang the next patient.

A woman answered in French.

'May I speak to Dr Karl Jacobs?'

'Dr Jacobs is on holiday. Can I take a message?'

'Well, perhaps you can tell me yourself if Dr Jacobs had any idea of the whereabouts of his analyst, Dr Hildegard Wolf? When will Dr Jacobs be back?'

'He's expected to return in about ten days. I can leave a message for him, but I don't think I can help. A gentleman called Walker has been asking how to get hold of Dr Wolf. He saw Dr Jacobs' name on the desk of the receptionist, I believe, as he was one of Dr Wolf's patients himself. Dr Wolf left suddenly, it seems.'

'Is Dr Jacobs upset?'

'Oh, no, he was very relieved. He said he'd had enough of her.'

Jean-Pierre left his phone number.

The next patient, Dr Oscar Hertz, was the one that Dominique had mentioned that Hildegard had liked. A widower, she had said; his problem, grief.

From Dr Oscar Hertz there was no reply. Jean-Pierre rang Mrs William Hane-Busby's number.

'Yes, speaking,' said the lady in the English tongue.

'I'm a friend of Dr Hildegard Wolf, and I have your name as one of her friends. You see I'm trying to find out where she is.'

'Yes, I would like to know, too. I esteem Dr Wolf greatly. A very distinguished mind. You know she is discussed in the universities and their publications. She must have had some very urgent reason for going off like that. Do you know her well?'

'She's my girl-friend,' Jean-Pierre felt it right to say. He liked this woman's tone.

'She often spoke to me of places she stayed in different parts, you know in Madrid she stayed at a lovely little hotel, the Paradiso, and at Zürich there was a gem of a place she loved, Seelach Gasthof, just a boarding-house really. She loved to stay in places like that, but perhaps she's with friends.'

'Where else did she mention, Madame? London? Brussels?'

'There was a place in London at Queen's Gate, and Brussels I don't know the name, it was a run-down part. She ate at a restaurant called La Moule Parquée, whatever that means. Oh, I do hope you can find her. I very much miss Hildegard. Why ever did she go off just like that?'

'Look,' said Jean-Pierre, 'I'll keep in touch. If she gets hold of you at all will you let me know?' He left his number.

He rang Dick and Paul. Dick answered. 'We were devastated when we got her message. Just a few lines enclosing a cheque and, although we're fully paid up, it kind of hurts. Do you know when she's coming back, Jean-Pierre? Did she leave any message with Olivia?'

Olivia, the maid whom Jean-Pierre and Hildegard had shared, was still working in the flat. She had already expressed herself as bewildered as everyone else by Hildegard's disappearance.

Jean-Pierre looked at the piece of paper where he had jotted down Mrs William Hane-Busby's information. She had been the only one to furnish any sort of clue as to where Hildegard might be. She had obviously been a confidante as much as a patient. Jean-Pierre put a cross against the Hotel Paradiso, Madrid, and a query against Hotel—, Queen's Gate, London. Maybe Brussels, though. He tried Dr Oscar Hertz's number again. This time he was more successful. A woman answered in guttural English, 'Dr Hertz? – I think he's just come in. Hold on.' A rendering of *Greensleeves* filled in the gap. It was cut off, not before time, by a click and a man's voice. 'Here is Dr Hertz.'

'I'm Jean-Pierre Roget, Hildegard Wolf's companion. I suppose you know she has disappeared.'

'I myself am very anxious about that.'

'If you're so anxious why didn't you telephone me? You know we lived together. You know that.'

'The secretary, Dominique, informed me. There is nothing we can do?'

'Dr Hertz, she had a special friendship with you. She –'

'Oh, yes, I was not a patient.'

'No?'

'No. I was a colleague.'

'You're a psychiatrist?'

'A psychologist, rather. Hildegard was not herself a theorist, she was essentially a practitioner.'

'You speak of her in the past tense.'

'Yes, I speak in the past tense.'

'Oh, God, what do you think has happened to her?'

'Nothing. She wasn't a person to whom things happen. She did all the happenings.'

'You think she's committed suicide on us?'

'I daresay.'

'Well, I daresay you're wrong. I know her better than you do.'

'She was being blackmailed.'

'That I know. And her disappearance is no doubt the result. But she has gone somewhere. Have you any idea where?'

'From a psychological point of view, if she remains alive she would be expected to have gone back to the place of her origin, to the countryside of Nuremberg. There, the most successful psychiatrist would be safe from detection.'

'Thank you, Dr Hertz.'

Jean-Pierre poured himself another drink. 'Cold bastard,' he reflected. He thought of Hertz's words: *From a psychological point of view . . . she would be expected . . .* As if Hildegard herself would not know what she might be expected to do, and avoid just that course of action. Jean-Pierre studied the few scribbles he had made on the telephone pad during his conversations. Certainly the cross he had made against Mrs William Hane-Busby's remarks was the most sensible, although he reserved suspicions about Dr Hertz. The houseboys, Dick and Paul, were probably reticent. Dr Jacobs, whoever he was, perhaps knew more than he would say if he were available. In the meantime Jean-Pierre busied himself in finding out the phone number of Hotel Paradiso, Madrid, the names of hotels, large and small, in Brussels, and in the Queen's Gate area of London.

*

Hildegard lay on top of her hotel bed aware of the pouring rain of London, which was somehow much worse than the equivalent rain of Paris. Her mind, with the passing of the years, had become ever more studious. It was not only because she feared the Lucan pair, but because she was fascinated by them, that she had brought, in her bulging zip-bags, the Lucan files comprising her notes and three published books on the subject of Lucan the killer, his habits of life, his *milieu*, his friends.

The documents were spread on the bed beside her, that double bed in which Hildegard had felt, every night she had spent in the Manderville Hotel, decidedly alone. Her lover had been replaced by her clinical notes.

She kept in touch with her *au pair* helpers in Paris, Dick and Paul. Yes, Jean-Pierre rang every day to find out if either one of them had heard from her. 'No, don't worry, we haven't said a word.' 'Once, that Mr Walker called. No one by name of Lucan.' 'Jean-Pierre is really frantic, though, Hildegard, why don't you call him?'

'I will,' Hildegard said, 'oh, yes, I will.' Eventually . . . she said to herself.

'Walker-Lucan', as she thought of him, had said to her, 'You know I am officially dead in England, although that leaves a big doubt as to the reality of my death. The House of Lords cannot recognise my death. Sometimes I'm tempted to go back, though, and challenge the courts. I would plead that, as a dead man, I couldn't be tried.'

'It wouldn't work,' said Hildegard. 'You would be tried for murder if you are indeed Lord Lucan.'

'Are you sure?'

'Yes, I am. And you would be found guilty on the evidence.'

'And you, Dr Wolf? On the evidence against you, could you still be tried for fraud?'

'Yes,' said Hildegard.

'All those years ago?'

'In both cases,' Hildegard said, 'all those years ago.'

Conversations like these led Hildegard to wonder if, after all, Walker was the real Lucan. He seemed to have been there at the kill.

But so, in a sense, through immersing herself in the subject, did she. And what interested her even more was the whole world of feelings that preceded Lucan's decision – apparently a good month before the event – to kill his wife. Hildegard opened one of her notebooks and read:

He detested his wife. She had defeated his law suit for the custody of his children, leaving him with a large legal debt and the mortification of being exposed by her as a sexual sadist, a wife-caner. In his eyes, his wife, Veronica, was expendable.

It was, according to the testimony, early in October 1974 that he actually told a friend of his decision to murder his wife, and of his carefully planned precautions. 'I would never be caught,' he told his friend (according to Chief Superintendent Ranson who conducted the investigation into the crime).

Twenty years later Ranson wrote, 'I believe that, rather than the much-quoted love of his children, it is his lack of money, all of it lost through uncontrollable gambling, that provides the key to this case.'

'I believe,' Hildegard had noted, 'that this is very much to the point, if not altogether true. Another motive is spite.'

'Walker,' Hildegard had also put in her notes, 'could be a hitman hired by Lucan, and Lucky is Lucan himself. Or it could be the other way round. But the evidence is all against this theory.'

Lucky, by Walker's account, genuinely needed treatment by a psychiatrist. Not long after Walker started consulting Hildegard he had said, 'I hear voices.'

By this he probably meant that Lucky 'heard' voices, and equally he was covering the personage of Lord Lucan for a possible confrontation with the law. Establish the 'voices' and Lucan could be found not fit to plead.

But was he fit to plead? Lucky, more so than Walker, Hildegard felt. But there was no doubt that in the weeks before the murder a certain madness had set in. 'Uncontrollable gambling', as the worthy policeman had cited as the main cause of his action, was in itself only a symptom. His hatred of his wife had been an obsession aggravated by the continual dunning letters from the banks to which he owed money.

Hildegard turned the pages of the Chief Superintendent's account. A year before the murder, letters from the bank managers were moving in on Lucan daily. These letters sounded like the phrases of a popular music-hall song:

23rd October 1973

Dear Lord Lucan,

I am extremely disappointed that I cannot trace a reply from you to my letter of the 10th October regarding the borrowing on your account . . .

And in December 1973, as his thirty-ninth birthday approached:

Dear Lord Lucan,

You will know from my recent letters how disappointed I am that you have not been in touch before this to let me know what arrangements are being made to adjust your overdraft here . . .

Lucan put the family silver up to auction at Christie's. He took recourse to money-lenders. Where, demanded Hildegard, did he say goodbye to reality? That he did just that is the only certainty in the case. For even if his plan had come off, even if he had succeeded in killing his wife and not the nanny, he could not have escaped detection. Was it the approach of his fortieth birthday combined with the shock of being a failure in life, irretrievably on the point of bankruptcy, that had removed him from reality? In the second half of the twentieth century, in any case, an inherited earldom was not very real. While it was a social fact, it did not relate to any other social fact of significance, especially in his case where there was little family property, no house with its land, no money. In reality, he belonged to a middle-class environment with upper-class claims in his conscious mind.

'He should have had a trade, a profession,' Hildegard said to herself. 'The calling of a gambler is madness. Being an earl, full stop, is madness. Yes, he needed the help of a psychiatrist. He still needs one. He needs me.'

Hildegard's notebooks were based on the published facts in the first place, and what Lucky had told her in the second.

Lucan had been married eleven years when the murder of the nanny and the savage attack on his wife took place that night at Lower Belgrave Street. He was separated from his wife. He had lost custody of his children. One way and another he had lost his mind. The jury at the dead girl's inquest pronounced her cause of death as 'Murder by Lord Lucan'. This was not itself a trial verdict, but it is impossible to conceive any other jury, on the known evidence, failing to convict him of murder. It is difficult to believe that his friends and family objectively believed his innocence, on the basis of the facts. To protest his innocence in public was the easiest thing he could have done. He had only to step forward and present his case. Surely there would have been some factors in his favour unknown to the investigators if he had not committed the crimes. His wife, covered with blood, had escaped to the nearby pub, from where she was taken to hospital with head injuries. They were inflicted, she said, by Lord Lucan, and the police believed her. They had every reason, with so much corroborative evidence, to believe her.

If Hildegard had only read about Lucan, and never met the probable man himself, she would have assumed that he was, like many obsessive gamblers, block-stupid.

The Lucky Lucan she knew, the Walker-Lucan she knew, were not stupid. Lucan's mind must anyway have been sharpened by constant evasion. Hildegard was conscious that Lucky Lucan, however, had a mental problem. Walker, to her, was probably a plain criminal. She remembered Lucan's loud laugh when he had made one of his jocular remarks. It was a laugh that filled the whole room. At her little jokes he merely gave a smile as if he were anxious about a waste of his time. Although he wore a smile, Walker seldom laughed, and if he did, it was a short, sharp, cynical 'huh'.

Walker had said he 'heard' voices.

What did they say?

'That Lucky is plotting to kill me.'

'But you didn't believe the voices, or you would not have come to consult me.'

'In fact there was only one voice.'

'Male or female?'

'A female voice. I think it was the murdered girl, Sandra Rivett, who spoke.'

In the margin of the page where she had transcribed her recording of this interview, Hildegard had noted: 'It is possible there is no "voice". It is poss. that Walker intends to kill Lucky and is establishing a cover-up of insanity in case he is caught. It is possible – but anything is poss.'

Hildegard added: 'Who is supporting these men? Who aided Lucan in the first place? Who aids and abets him now? He has friends somewhere.'

In the matter of the seventh Lord Lucan's disappearance the public was more mystified than outraged. The more he was described, and his way of life outlined, by his friends, the less he was understood. The case of the seventh Earl is only secondarily one of an evasion of justice, it is primarily that of a mystery. And it is not only the question of how did he get away, where did he go, how has he been living, is he in fact alive? The mystery is even more in the question of what was he like, how did he feel, what went on in his mind that led him to believe he could get away with his plan? What detective stories had he been reading? What dream-like, immature culture was he influenced by? For, surely, he had thought his plan to kill his wife was watertight. Whereas, even if the nanny had taken her night off, even if he had murdered the countess, the plot leaked at every seam as truly as did the blood-oozing mailbag into which the body of Sandra Rivett was packed.

12

As Hildegard knew from her own experience as a stigmatic fraud, blood, once let loose, gets all over the place. It sticks, it flows, it garishly advertises itself or accumulates in dark thick puddles. Once it gets going, there is no stopping blood.

It was a description by Lucky, finally, of the blood all over his trousers, of the blood oozing from the mailbag, that had inclined Hildegard to believe that he was indeed the Lucan who was wanted for homicide. Walker, on the other hand, was reluctant to describe the murder. He had now told Hildegard that, yes, he had 'performed the deed', and he had even gone into some of the already well-publicised details. Walker sometimes sounded like a printed column out of a tabloid Sunday edition. 'I thought it convenient at that stage to rid myself of a wife that I had come to loathe. She had custody of my children. A ridiculous member of your profession, Dr Wolf, gave evidence in her favour in a court of law. I lost my children. I was allowed to see them twice a month – imagine! I could have sold the house at Lower Belgrave Street to pay off some of my debts. She was mad, but the court would not recognise it.'

'Tell me about the murder.'

'Oh, I suppose it was a murder like any other murder.'

Perhaps these were the words of a hit-man. Perhaps and maybe. But, Hildegard noted, they were hardly a killer's words. And yet, their coldness might fit in with the Lucan known to the public, his mad-cold calculative mind.

But behind it all, at this stage, was blackmail. Blackmail between Lucan and Walker, with Walker the probable blackmailer, and now blackmail of herself: they needed money. What else did they need? Probably a psychiatrist's counselling and comfort? – Yes, probably that, too. And perhaps a sympathetic psychiatrist to testify in the event of a court case.

The last witness to see Lucan after the murder gave evidence at the inquest on the death of Sandra Rivett that Lucan had told her how an unknown intruder had attacked his wife and presumably killed the nanny, he himself having passed the house by chance and intervened. According to the witness, she had the impression that he 'felt rather squeamish about the blood and did not want to look too closely at the sack'.

All right, Lucky was squeamish. Hildegard's story, also dripping in blood, had evidently given him further reason for his squeams. 'You covered your hands, side and feet with your menstrual blood, Dr Wolf.' He had found the courage to come out with that statement, squeamish or not. He had said it in an almost confidential way: we're both in this blood-business together, he seemed to say. Walker, however, had merely referred to 'Your past, Hildegard Wolf or should I say Beate Pappenheim?'

When Lucky had first walked into her office, Hildegard was immediately taken with his resemblance to her prior Lucan patient, Walker. They were not indistinguishable, but they might have been brothers. And certainly, both were white-haired, ageing photos of the thirty-nine-year-old Lucan which looked out of the pages of the quantity of books and press articles written about him from year to year since his disappearance in 1974. Was the real Lucan dead, as numerous people claimed? If he wasn't, how did he materially survive? Walker himself had never claimed that he presented himself to Lucan's friends. It was usually Lucky who periodically collected sums of money, deposited at certain places, with certain people, by rich friends. Friends – how could they be deceived if they had once known Lucan? 'Easy,' Walker had explained. 'They expect Lucan to have undergone surgical modifications to his features. They are right. Your other Lucan patient is a fraud, Dr Wolf. He also goes collecting, as you can imagine.'

'But you work together.'

'Of course. If one of us were caught, it would always be the other, the absent Lucan who would be the real one.'

'And your voices? Don't your friends suspect from the voice?'

'Lucan is known to be musical. We have coordinated our voices. Besides, people might assume that voices change.'

Years ago, there had been an arrest. Lucan is found in Australia! Indeed the suspect turned out to be a very-much-wanted missing man; but he wasn't Lucan. And as far as Hildegard was concerned, neither, as yet, were quite proved to be either Walker or Lucky. She had a naturally objective set of wits. The men were each, to her, 'a mere anatomy, a mountebank . . . a living-dead man', as Shakespeare had put it long ago.

In manners, in speech, Hildegard had written, both Lucky and Walker could have based themselves on the Lucan of the historical case. Their methods of copying would have been fairly easy for the reason that Lucan himself had been a perfect bore, a cut-to-measure gentleman with a pack of memories very, very like that of many another man of his class and education. He does not appear to have had one original idea, ever, beyond that of attempting and planning to murder his wife. He was extremely average of mind. He could have been anybody. With a smattering of information about the past life and schooling of a man like Lucan, given the height and shape, it would not have been difficult to assume a personality that would convince his acquaintances of his identity. Oh, Lucan, Lucan, you hot potato.

The rain had stopped. Hildegard put away her notes. She felt a great longing for Jean-Pierre and regretted not being connected even by e-mail. Surely he would be looking for her, might even find her. But she didn't trust his tact in evading the Lucans. Jean-Pierre lacked duplicity whereas they were altogether a double proposition. Sooner or later she would phone him.

13

Walker had a very fixed idea of what a gentleman should be. He had studied Lucky Lucan diligently for ten of the years since Lucan had been a wanted man on the loose. He had got most of his ideas about a hundred years out of date, as were the convictions and attitudes of Lucan himself, for Lucan's conceptions of a gentleman were greatly distorted. This had been noted by his fellow guardsmen in the Coldstream regiment, where Lucan played the Earl from start to finish, outdoing the other earls in the practice of earldom.

Walker's notion of a gentleman was further distorted by the reality of Lucan's character. Lucan was, in fact, bent, a natural felon, a failed person. He was self-centred as a man, self-occupied as a nobleman; the mask of the upstart, strangely, was Lord Lucan's favourite mode of self-expression. 'Virtue and honour': his family specifically claimed that these were guiding features of their fugitive kinsman. However, they were obviously not remotely attributes of his; they were the façade which Walker in his role of freelance gentleman had assiduously copied and assumed. Yes, he was now ideally Lucan's doppelgänger, his other self.

Walker's physical resemblance to Lucan had grown over those years since they had met in Mexico. Its initial advantage was the two men's precisely identical height of six-foot-plus and the curious melon-like shape of their heads. Lucan's head was described by an acquaintance as 'bony', and so was Walker's. Their dark colouring had been more or less the same. Only their separate features had differed. This had been attended to gradually in the more recent years by plastic surgery, so that it was now fairly difficult to tell the two men apart.

Lucan, however, had a certain charm, not a great deal of it, but enough to be all the more charming. Walker had none and was always at a loss how to achieve it; was transparent, which at times was in itself quite appealing. Where they resembled each other most in character was in their aptitude for cold indifference; on that level they never failed to be in harmony.

Walker had come to Lucan's notice on a ranch in Mexico, one of Lucan's many places of refuge in the years following his disappearance. His host had been a small spare man, nut-brown, a horse-racing old-time friend; the hostess had been an actress from Bolivia, now retired into a life of retaining her wonderful looks day by day, and keeping her clothes, which she changed frequently, fresh and ironed all the time.

'It's remarkable,' she said, 'how much Walker resembles you. I thought he was you last night when he walked across the lawn to the house.'

'So strange,' said the host, 'I thought so too.'

After two months it was nearly time for Lucan to move on to his next aiders and abetters.

'I will give you Walker,' said the kindly Mexican. 'You may take Walker with you. He'll come in useful.'

Walker was a butler-keeper and head groom (for the establishment was constituted on hierarchical lines).

'I don't know,' said his wife, 'if I can manage without Walker.'

'I give him to Lucan,' said the man, very casually, as if he was presenting the Earl with a silver dish.

'What should I do with him?' said Lucan the comparative blockhead.

'You can use him a thousand ways,' said the all-knowing, all-experienced host. 'He could be arrested in your place, if necessary. You must train him up a bit, make him more your double, teach him your voice.'

'He is very intelligent,' said the wife.

'If he was very intelligent,' said the sage brown fellow, 'he wouldn't be working for us. However, he will do as I say. Besides,' he said wearily, 'I will of course make it worth his while. I give him to Lucan. Get his chin modified, Lucan, and his nose straightened a bit. He's the very image.'

That had been ten years ago. Walker had not needed to make frequent trips to Mexico to collect his former employer's bounty. Unlike Lucan, he was safe with bank transfers. As Walker, no one was looking for him, although as Lucan he had several times fallen under suspicion. As Lucan he had been 'sighted' on the beaches of the world, in cafés. He had been a temporary secretary of a sports club in Sydney, and sighted there. He had been a riding instructor at a school at Lausanne, from where he had to flee from a 'sighting'. Interpol never caught up with him, and if they had, he was, after all, Walker, with Walker's passport, Walker's birth certificate, Walker's own blood group. Lucan, meanwhile, was always elsewhere, in and out of jobs, or lounging in hotel gardens. He painfully avoided the casinos, where he knew he would be looked for.

The Mexican was not his only patron, but he was the richest. When he died in 1998, Lucan was left with only two firm friends of the past, the actress–wife having cut off

Walker's allowance and Lucan's hand-outs without explanation. Walker and Lucan went to Paris.

Lucan was always anxious about Walker's voice. Walker had adopted the slightly plummy full-fruited accents of Lucan's speech, but still it was not quite right. Lucan knew that although Walker's looks could pass for a twenty-year-later Lucan with his old friends, the voice, perhaps, could not. So far, he preferred to go 'collecting' by himself.

But money was getting short for both of them. Walker made it plain to Lucan that they were not, ever, to separate. By the time they hit on Hildegard and her past, they needed her more for genuine psychiatric help than for what she could yield through blackmail.

Lucan, in Scotland for his latest collecting venture, received a phone call from Walker.

'Don't think,' said Walker, 'don't so much as let it cross your mind to fail to return to Paris. I need you here.'

Lucan said, 'I'm coming to Paris.' In fact he had nowhere else to go. He hated Walker, but there was no escape from him. And now he had begun to find out more about Walker, who knew so much, so very much, about him, if only through those books and articles that had probed every aspect of his past life.

Walker and Lucan, Lucan and Walker, they were bound together.

Walker, for his part, could hardly bear to look at Lucan's melon-shaped head, exactly like his own.

There was one enormous difference between them, however, and both knew it. Lucan was a killer and Walker was not.

Lucky Lucan believed in destiny. By virtue of destiny he was an earl. His wife had been destined to die, according to his mad calculation. It was the madness of a gambler. During the last two months before the attempt on his wife, Lucan had behaved with comparative civility towards her; even, it was reported, with tenderness. He understood she was destined to die and did not for one moment reflect that this destiny arose merely from his own calculations and plans. His 'needs' dictated fate itself. He had 'needed' the money that would have derived from the sale of the house she occupied, he 'needed' his wife dead, and it was destiny.

It was also now his destiny to share his life with Walker. But an overriding 'need' had arisen. Old friends were dying or dropping off. Lucan needed to rid himself of Walker, and soon; before Walker decided that Lucan must die, it was Walker's destiny to die.

On the plane to Paris, Lucan began to work out the mechanics of Walker's death. Walker was a card to be played in this gambling-den of life; not an ace card, merely a card. It was a situation in which Lucan felt confident, with the sort of confidence with which he had felt he could kill his wife with impunity. His feelings were those of a gambler. His confidence was a card-player's. His sense of destiny obliterated the constant, well-known fact that the gambler loses and the bookie, the croupier or whoever, always wins in the end. Walker was a card to be played, and there was no intention in Lucan's mind generously to share his latest 'collected' windfall with his look-alike. This latest bundle of luck might well be the last, these days being these days.

Walker must go. The stewardess brought him a glass, a half-bottle of flat Vichy water and a miniature Johnnie Walker which Lucan twirled in his fingers with some scorn, before opening and pouring. Presently she returned, offering him a plastic meal which he refused.

Walker must go, die, disintegrate. By habit Lucan wore tinted glasses; they had no special lens: his contact lenses, a messy brown colour, disguising his blue eyes, were made for his natural vision. He was in business class and sat in the aisle seat, which he always preferred. It gave him the feeling of a quick getaway, even on a plane. Twenty-five years had not settled his jitters. No years would do that. If he had remained at home and faced his trial and certain conviction, under the two charges against him, he would by now have been a free man for at least ten years, a fact which he appreciated but did not ponder. There had been no question of his standing trial. He was the seventh Earl of Lucan. He had never got used to, or understood, the casual treatment, often contempt, that had been slung his way in the press by his peers. Not one of the other earls, even those of his schooldays or his regimental years, had spoken up for him. Besides most of his immediate family, which was understandable, only his gambling friends and his less nobly born friends had expressed horror at his plight; they had done their best.

By habit Lucan scrutinised, with more than usual passenger-curiosity, the other travellers. Beside him was a girl with long streaky hair, reading *Newsweek* while picking into her tray of food. She, yes, could be a detective. Had they stopped looking for him? He could never be sure. This trip to England would have to be his last. With modern technology collecting was becoming too dangerous and the collection itself too meagre. He took out his book, a detective paperback. For twenty-five years he had been taking out paperbacks on planes and buses, remembering always to turn the pages regularly, even when his glances were elsewhere. His jitters at all times: he felt he did not deserve such a fate. He hadn't killed his wife, after all. Only the girl with all that blood. He turned a page and sighed. His neighbour read and picked on.

Across the aisle, on his left, were a couple of men, one older than the other. They, too, were busy with their drinks, talking together quite softly but audibly. Lucan disliked homosexuals; what he disliked most about them was what he claimed to be their sentimentality. No ruthlessness; no sense of destiny; no idea that what had to be done had to be done, like the murder. It was a blunder but it was destiny, it was the throw of the dice. The couple beside him across the aisle were a man of about fifty and one of about twenty-five. The older man had shoulder-length hair. The younger had a close-cropped head and was bedecked with worked-silver earrings. They were discussing a film. (Gone were the days when it happened to Lucan that he would overhear people at the next table, in a bus or a waiting-room, discussing him.)

'It was all too obvious,' said the older man. 'All you had to do after the half-way mark, more or less, was sit through it to the end.'

'I thought the sex scenes kind of cool,' observed the younger man.

'Did you? I thought they looked contrived. They did it in their underpants.'

The hostess came along with their trays and they started to eat in the silence due to the task.

Suddenly, from the seat in front of them, the seat diagonally in front of Lucan's to the left, came the electric word 'Lucan', quite discernible amongst the patchy fuzz of their conversation. A bald man of about sixty with a pretty fair-haired woman in her thirties. Lucan released his seatbelt; he stood up and out into the aisle to see them more clearly from the height of his 6´ 2". They had a large quantity of newspaper cuttings on the table in front of them. Yes, indeed, they were all old cuttings, some from the long past, all about him.

LUCAN DISAPPEARS
BODY FOUND IN US MAIL SACK
WHO KILLED SANDRA RIVETT?
COUNTESS BLEEDING IN HOSPITAL
LUCAN AT LARGE

Lucan went to the lavatory, came back and settled in his seat. By this time the couple had put away their papers and were eating their meal with a good deal of appetite.

Good God, it is Joe Murray – or is it? Yes, he would be about that age now. Clearly it was Joe, who had been at St Columba's monastery with his girlfriend, Maria Twickenham's daughter, snooping into his whereabouts. It was Joe and this girl who had trailed him down from the north up to the gates of the house with that fortuitous wedding. Yes, it was them. Ambrose had said he'd given them cuttings, bloody fool. Lucan now applied himself to his book, turning pages at due intervals.

Lucan had brought only hand-luggage. As soon as the plane stopped and the passengers were allowed to shuffle out, he reached up into the baggage compartment and fetched down his bag. He hastened.

'Funny,' said Joe to Lacey, as they followed the tall dark-spectacled fellow to the exit, 'how, if you concentrate on a subject, you seem to see examples of it all over the place. I could have sworn that the man along there, three people in front, resembled Lucan. But of course . . .'

Lacey had to tiptoe to see the indicated passenger. So many of the people now pushing up to the exit or reaching for their luggage in the upper compartments were, it seemed to her, excessively big, blocking her view of the possible Lucan. What she managed to see were hefty people, men and women. One of the men was wearing dark glasses, but as soon as he had pulled down his bag he took them off and put them in his breast pocket; hardly the gesture of a Lucan wishing to hide himself.

Lucan was already on the Paris Centre-bound bus by the time Joe and Lacey retrieved their luggage from the round-about. It was only then that Joe, standing still, said, 'Lacey, you know I believe that man in the plane was Lucan. He caught my eye very rapidly, you know; I think he recognised me; and yes, I recognised him, I really did. But too late; what an old fool I am.'

'We could have had him stopped, even arrested, right there on the plane,' said Lacey. 'The captain has the power to do that.'

'I wouldn't really have cared to call the captain,' said Joe. 'Suppose we'd been mistaken?'

'But aren't you sure?'

'In fact, yes, I'm sure. It's difficult to say what one would do.'

'Oh, Joe,' she said, lifting her luggage and ready to move off with it, 'I thought you wanted to help me.'

'Yes, I do.' He looked round the crowded hall. 'He's gone, of course. Gone. We'll find him in Paris, maybe, though. At least we're almost sure he's in Paris, now.'

'Oh, Paris,' said Lacey. 'Come on, let's get a taxi.'

14

Jean-Pierre, in his ample, cluttered workshop, was restoring a gramophone of the 1920s for someone with more money than sense, when a tall black young man came to the glass door and rang. Jean-Pierre sometimes kept this door locked even when he was inside, with the shutters up; the area was a rough one.

Jean-Pierre opened the door to this decidedly tranquil customer.

'We've been on the phone,' said the man in English. 'I'm Dr Karl K. Jacobs, patient of Dr Hildegard Wolf.'

'Come in.'

'You rang me up.'

'Yes, I know. You said you were fed up with Hildegard; something like that. Have you any news of her?' Jean-Pierre moved a pile of old magazines and catalogues off a chair, and pushed it with a foot towards Dr Jacobs. 'Sit down.' He himself sat opposite on a rickety work-stool.

'I had enough,' said Jacobs. 'She was always talking about herself, enquiring about the voodoo cults of the Congo, the medicine-men. I had enough interrogation. The concierge at the rue du Dragon told me where your shop is.'

'*Enough*, but you've come for more?' said Jean-Pierre.

'What do you want to know?'

'What do *you* want to know?'

'Where she is,' said Karl Jacobs. 'I was recommended to consult her but all she has done is consult me. Then – off.'

'That's her way.'

'She not only consults, she insults. She wants to needle me, reminding me always of my background as she thinks it is. I come from the centre of Africa but I haven't just walked out of the jungle. What about the voodoos, the witch doctors? she wanted to know. How should I know about the medicine-men, all those frauds? I am a qualified MD.'

'Where do you work?' said Jean-Pierre.

'I'm at a private nursing-home north of Versailles, I live near the Marais. I get in and out by autobus, sometimes I use the metro and change. What have I got to do with jungle magic and blood rites?'

'Blood rites?'

'Yes, blood is important in these activities. Why does she worry me?'

'That's something between you and her,' said Jean-Pierre. 'I can offer you a cup of instant coffee or a glass of wine.'

'Wine.'

'I know,' said Jean-Pierre as he poured two glasses of red wine, 'that Hildegard is interested in superstitions.'

'Yes, but why should she be interested at my expense? I paid her for those sessions. I have my own problems.'

'Psychiatrists have their methods, you know,' said Jean-Pierre.

'But I paid her for her advice.'

'Women are expensive,' said Jean-Pierre. 'Look – I'm trying to trace her whereabouts, I don't deny. Do you have any clue where she might be?'

'London.'

'Why do you say London?'

'It's where I'd go if I wanted to hide.'

'How do you know she wants to hide?'

Karl Jacobs was neatly dressed in a dark business suit, a blue shirt with a white collar, and a grey striped tie with dark-blue dots. He sat with his long legs stretched forth. An effortlessly athletic man. Jean-Pierre repeated his question, 'Why should she hide?'

'Her interest in voodoo, in blood cults and fraudulent mystifications was very genuine. I think it was probably personal. She could be connected with someone like that.'

'Do you know anything, Dr Jacobs, about these practices?'

'Call me Karl. My name is Karl Kanzia Jacobs. My father was a judge, he's dead. My mother is alive. She is a very important citizen of Kanzia.'

'And Kanzia is where?'

'It's an independent entity of central Africa, slightly north of the equator.'

'But certainly they wouldn't have any witchery and magic there, I imagine,' ventured Jean-Pierre.

'Oh, indirectly, I know something. My grandfather Delihu is still a paramount head man. My uncle was a voodoo chap, he died. He was definitely what you would call in your terms a witch doctor. He performed great good, especially with rites and totems and herbs and of course the terror of beliefs. Beliefs are essential. I can confirm as a medical man that these witch men can cure, but there is also a lot of mumbo-jumbo, like you say. It's a question of cutting a fine line, Jean-Pierre, and Dr Wolf was interested in that aspect, the question of responsibility on the part of the self-styled healer. Myself, I feel it is a treachery to scientific practices to agree with her. And yet . . . She said, if a cure is effected does it matter whether or not there was an actual miracle to cause it? Why should the healer be prosecuted, or at least blamed, if in fact he heals? She put that very question to me. I told her no. I told her there should be no blame, but all this was at the expense of my pocket. I paid for those sessions.'

'Perhaps I can reimburse you on her behalf?'

'Certainly not.'

'But surely,' said Jean-Pierre, 'it is always worthwhile conversing with Hildegard? If it isn't, what are you doing here?'

'She is very fascinating,' said Karl Jacobs, gloomily.

Jean-Pierre asked if they might keep in touch, and assured Karl that once Hildegard returned, as surely she would, he would see to it that she would give him the full sessions he was due. 'If you have any other brainwaves or intuitions about where she has gone,' said Jean-Pierre, 'call me at once. I intend to have her back. She's my girlfriend and my life-companion of more than five years and I can't live without her. London might well be the place. I'll work on that.'

When Karl had gone, Jean-Pierre took out of his pocket the sheet of paper on which he had made notes of all the replies to his enquiries of Hildegard's patients. He scribbled the word 'promising' beside the name of Dr Karl K. Jacobs. Then he studied the list again. Only one name, of course, was equally promising: that of Mrs William Hane-Busby.

Madrid – The Paradiso – he had already called there without success.

Seelach Gasthof – there were so many guest-houses which could fit that description. However, none of them had yielded Hildegard. Then London. 'London is where I'd hide,' Jacobs had said with a quite definite tone. 'London at Queen's Gate . . .' Mrs Hane-Busby had mused.

Jean-Pierre decided to hunt up in the directories all the hotels and boarding-houses at Queen's Gate, London. It was only five-thirty in the afternoon, but he shut up shop.

15

Hildegard lay in her bath trying to trace back the source of a slightly disconsolate and disagreeable sensation that lingered over from the day. It was six-thirty p.m. The best feature of the hotel was its constant, really hot water; Hildegard profited by it frequently before dinner: the soothing power of a hot bath. What was her feeling of uneasiness due to? She had left the hotel that morning at ten and taken a bus to Marble Arch. From there she went to several department stores in a leisurely way all along Oxford Street. Hildegard had brought few clothes with her, and now she was beginning to need a change. Gradually, that morning, she had acquired a woollen jacket, a pair of suede boots, four pairs of nylon tights, a pair of brown jeans, a brown cotton shirt and a bottle of English toilet spray called *Amours de Boudoir*. It was here that Hildegard's pondering in the bath was arrested. Walking along the ground-floor aisles of the shops that afternoon, she was reminded of her days as a student, earning a poor living from a part-time job at the handbag counter of a department store in Munich. At the cosmetics counter, Hildegard had stopped to try the toilet-water samples being offered by a young woman. It seemed to Hildegard that this woman looked away, and looked again and looked away. Hildegard was taken back to the store of her youth. It was the cosmetics girl who had unwittingly given her the idea of assuming the false stigmata.

The cosmetics girl, Ursula, could make up and transform the most ordinary faces. Hildegard had been fascinated. Ursula did a romantic scar, one day, on the left cheek of a young man who happily said he was going to pose as having been involved in a duel.

Ursula, when the time came, made a deep, false indentation in the palm of Hildegard's hand. Hildegard, then Beate Pappenheim at the height of her success, would get Ursula to come around each month at the time of her menstruation and put the touches of reality on her 'five wounds' so that they could be photographed.

Could that young woman in the department store in Oxford Street be really Ursula? She looked so like Ursula, it was incredible, and then her furtive glances at Hildegard, her look, her look away, her look again, her look away . . . Did she recognise me? Hildegard asked herself.

And then she realised how perfectly ridiculous her idea had been. Ursula twelve years ago must have already been over thirty. Now she would be in her mid-forties, much older than the young woman in the department store of today. Hildegard, pulling her thoughts together, apprehended how she herself must have looked strangely at the girl in order to provoke the strange looks she returned. Hildegard had allowed herself to be sprayed by the scent, had bought some and left. *Amours de Boudoir* – oh, well . . .

All the same, Hildegard was aware that she could still be discovered, exposed. She felt more vulnerable in London than she had ever felt in Paris, perhaps because she looked very French with her dark short-cut hair clinging to her egg-shaped head? She had lost her German look simply by living in France, eating French food, breathing French air. Her skin was still pale, but her waistline small, which had not been so much the case when she had first fled from Munich. She mingled well in Paris, but in London?

'If you want to hide a pebble the best place is the beach' – an old and true maxim. Hildegard – or as she was, Beate – when the scandal broke took eventual refuge in Spain, at Avila, birthplace of two famous Catholic vision- aries, St Theresa of Jesus and St John of the Cross. Nobody thought of looking for her in that atmosphere of heated romantic ecstasy. She was considered to be a fraud. Nobody was looking for her at Avila where a truly holy stigmatic would be likely to linger. In fact she stayed in a convent at Avila for six months, impressing the nuns with her devotion and goodness, her daily visits to the cathedral, to the house of St Theresa, to the birthplace of St Theresa, and with her meditative walks in the shadow of Avila's great and ancient walls. After all, she had mused then (and, in her bath in her London hotel, mused now), I did apparently effect a number of cures, perhaps by the power of sugges- tion, it's true. But people were cured by me in my stigmatic days. I felt the part.

She wondered, then, if she would change her hair to fair. If one of the Lucans in fact caught up with her, she had better disguise herself a little.

Among the names of Lucan's friends published in newspa- pers in those days after the murder were those of Maria and Alfred Twickenham. Maria's interview with the police in South Africa, where she was at the time, was one of many; it obtained prominence largely through Maria's glamour and beauty. Her picture was a good accompaniment to the sensational articles. All the articles were by the nature of the case sensational. A peer was wanted for a brutal murder. He had bashed his children's nanny to death with a length of lead piping, specially prepared to deaden the thuds. Had there been a relationship with the nanny? No, there hadn't. Far from it, he had meant those thuds for his wife. Having removed the light-bulb on the basement staircase, he had mistaken the young nanny descending the stairs for his young wife. On discovering his blunder, he then attacked the wife, reported the papers. She was now in hospital with severe head wounds.

That night Lucan, in a panic, visited some of his friends. The main one in London was the late Alfred Twickenham. His ex-wife was probably still alive. Hildegard knew that all Lucan's other friends were either still in the country and no doubt not accessible to enquirers, or dead.

Hildegard in her anxiety to defend herself from Lucan and Walker with their threatening knowledge, and in an increasingly neurotic state from her confinement to a small London hotel, had still plenty of courage to take a decision. Apart from having her hair dyed a mild beige colour, she wanted to do more than just hide. Looking through the books that had been written on the Lucan case, she noted that all of them were generously illustrated by photographs: Lucan at Eton, Lucan's engagement portrait, Lucan with his friends in his favourite gaming clubs: oh, look at these people, look close. Hildegard was looking close: Doris McGuire, said the subtitle, Charles McGuire – Maria Twickenham. Yes, it was Maria Twickenham, who, according to the telephone directory, still lived in the same house in Lennox Gardens as her husband had occupied at the time of the murder.

Hildegard, with her talent for summoning up new fighting energy, was already on the offensive. She would hunt Lucan, threaten him if absolutely necessary; not he her.

She would chase Lucan, she would hunt him down, confront him, challenge him, dare him to reveal her secret.

'You are charged with the crime of murder and attempted murder,' she could say, 'and I am not. You haven't a chance, given the state of the evidence; you have no extenuating arguments to support you; I have.' And she thought: not to speak of my personal documents so carefully prepared in Marseilles.

It was a question, perhaps, of getting to know Maria Twickenham. That for a start.

Hildegard had now sat in her hired car near the house in Lennox Gardens frequently enough to realise that it was no longer the smart one-family residence of twenty-five years ago. It was still verging on smartness but it was broken up into flats. There had been a coming and going of men and women in their thirties, business-like and attractively dressed; they largely left home around nine a.m. and returned around six p.m. Some passed in and out about lunch time. A white-haired, large woman of about sixty, who might well have been an older version of Maria's photo-graph, dressed in a woolly jacket and trousers, emerged every morning and returned with at least one full shopping bag. She must be Maria Twickenham, thought Hildegard. But no, on following her with some difficulty to the nearby supermarket, Hildegard managed to squint at the name on her credit card. It wasn't Twickenham, Maria's name, the name in the phone book. It was Louise B. Wilson.

At least this waiting and watching and surreptitious stalk-ing was more to Hildegard's taste than the boring, very boring, daily brood in her hotel room. She set forth once again to sit near the white front door of the Twickenham house with its shining brass door-plates. It was Hildegard's fifth wait when a taxi pulled up, and a tall, thin woman in her sixties emerged from the house under the evening lamplight. She stepped into the cab. Hildegard followed as best she could, but lost it at a traffic-light. She felt sure it contained Maria.

Next morning, about eleven a.m., out stepped the large white-haired Louise B. Wilson again. Hildegard leapt out of her car and approached her. 'Excuse me,' she said. 'I wonder if you can tell me, are there any rooms or flats available in this house?'

'I wouldn't know really,' said the woman. 'I'm just the home-help for Mrs Twickenham. You'd have to ask her.'

'Is she in now?'

'Well, if you have any references. Do you have a reference – who sent you, I mean?'

'Yes, of course. I got the name and address from someone in Paris, where I live. I'm only here doing a university course for some months.'

The ground-floor flat had been reserved for Maria's own use, and Hildegard was asked in to wait while Louise B. Wilson went to make enquiries. In a warm, upholstered sitting-room Hildegard thought she saw in the large mirror over the mantelpiece another woman behind her. But on looking back, there was nobody. Of course, my blonde hair, Hildegard remembered. But this fragmentary episode put Hildegard in an ever more guarded and inventive frame of mind, so that when tall Maria came smiling into the room, Hildegard was ready with her plausible tongue.

'I was given your name by an old schoolfriend of yours in Paris.'

This is a tactic in the con-business that usually works. The mention of a schoolfriend one doesn't remember generally gives rise to a slight feeling of guilt rather than suspicion. Instead of a reaction like: 'This person is probably a fake. I don't know or remember any such schoolfriend,' it is more likely to be: 'My God, have I become so forgetful? Or so grand? Or so detached from my youth? Don't I remember who got married? Well, I don't really care about their fate.'

Maria said, in fact, 'I vaguely remember the name. What was her maiden name?'

'I think it was Singleton, but maybe not. She got married as you probably know into Carters' Publications, tall, brown-haired, extremely athletic. After her divorce, of course, she married someone else, I think. She remembered you so well and knows all about you here in London braving it out as you do. I'm sure you can recall . . .'

Hildegard had an address in Paris ready on her tongue, but it wasn't necessary. 'Yes, of course,' said Maria. 'Of course I remember her. And you'll have some coffee, won't you? I'm about to make some. Let's go into the kitchen.'

There she told Hildegard, yes, there would be a two-room flat on the fourth floor available from the week after next. The tenant was out at his job at the moment, and wouldn't mind her showing it to Hildegard. 'Will you be staying long in London?'

'I have to complete some research. I'm a psychiatrist.'

'How fascinating!' (They always said that.)

Like most people, Maria was intrigued by the thought of having a psychiatrist at hand to talk to, without actually taking the plunge of consulting one. There was nothing wrong with Maria, but she herself thought there was; in reality her problem was boredom.

This problem was about to be solved. Maria, although she really had quite a number of friends, had not for many years met anyone quite like Dr Wolf. Hildegard Wolf was the name on her passport and her fake birth certificate. She had not changed it while hiding in London, so that she would not appear to be hiding, if discovered. And it was much easier to deal with people under a name to which she was accustomed. So she was Dr Wolf ('call me Hildegard') to the enchanted landlady, Maria.

As they talked, Maria almost felt she could recall Hildegard's apocryphal Fay Singleton, so like was she, in any case, to the girls of her day.

'And, of course,' said Hildegard boldly, as the morning wore on, 'you knew Lucan, didn't you? Fay told me. It must have been a shock to find that someone you knew so well was wanted for murder.'

By now, they were in Maria's living room, drinks in hand. 'At one time, well, we couldn't believe it. Of course, I was away at the time. My late ex-husband and I believed it, yes, and yet we didn't. Now that we know more . . . And, after all, times have changed, and after all, Lucky Lucan failed to show up, which was really lowering our standards, we all feel different. Or nearly all of us who knew him of old. Most of my friends who knew Lucan now have a poor opinion of him. He might at least have stood trial. And we all feel, now, for poor Sandra Rivett's son, who was deprived of her so tragically without ever knowing her as a mother; she was supposed to be a sister. Poor girl. Of course, you know Lucky Lucan was a very great bore. I was too young to notice that he was a bore, if you know what I mean. He was just one of the chaps. Very good-looking. But I know someone who was at school with him, at Eton. He sat beside him in the choir. My dear, what a bore he thought Lucan was. And the same in the Guards.'

'Is he alive?' said Hildegard.

'I think so. Personally, I think so. Very few people do. But my daughter, Lacey, is actually trying to trace him. She's going to write a book. She's in Paris just now with Lucky's old friend, Joe Murray – he's the zoologist you've probably heard of – trying to track him down.' She took up a photograph and handed it to Hildegard. 'That's Lacey,' she said.

'How lovely,' said Hildegard quite justly.

'And intelligent, too,' said Maria.

16

Jean-Pierre's workshop was becoming a place of pilgrimage for Hildegard's abandoned patients.

Dr Hertz, a thin man in his mid-forties, of medium height and wearing tinted glasses, darkened the doors of Jean-Pierre's place two days after their conversation on the phone. He rang the bell, and Jean-Pierre opened the door.

'I'm Hertz.'

'Come in.'

'Have you heard from Hildegard?'

'Well, what if I have heard?'

'I want to know. I must know what has happened to her. I had a fixed appointment for this afternoon.'

'At her office?'

'Yes, of course.'

'Then you are a patient, after all.'

'You might say patient, you might say colleague. She confided in me. We speak in German.'

Jean-Pierre could have knifed him at that point, but in reality would not have done. He said, 'What do you know about Hildegard's youth?'

'Everything vital. I know she posed as a stigmatic. That I admire. I don't blame her for doing something constructive with her own blood. What else should a woman of imagination do with her menstrual blood? I am a psychologist. I see that now comes this Lucan with blood on his hands in a manner much worse, and his money supply is getting shaky, and his friends are no more, nearly all, and he has heard of Hildegard's activities. So he will expose her for her old crime.'

'And his old crime?' said Jean-Pierre.

'Lucan is elusive. Do you know Hildegard never knew his address in Paris? And in the end, he would turn out to be not Lucan but the other, that man Walker. They had lived on that evasive principle till a few years ago, my friend. Now we have DNA identification, it is more difficult for Lucan, and he is even more slippery.'

'What do you want with Hildegard?' Jean-Pierre said.

'I need her consolation. I am weeping over my dead wife, these three months.'

'I, too, need her consolation.'

'But I will marry her. You will not.'

'How do you know?'

'Because you haven't done so.'

'We've been together more than five years. She doesn't want marriage.'

'If I knew where she was I would go and find her. She could marry me. We have a profession in common.' Hertz looked round the workshop. Jean-Pierre had on his work-bench a wooden model of Milan's ornate cathedral, inset with ivory. It was a very elaborate affair. Jean-Pierre was restoring it. The tiny pincers and pieces of ivory lay ready beside the model edifice. Jean-Pierre knew what Hertz was saying with his look: 'She can't be satisfied fully with a companion who is merely an artisan. I am her equal, a professional man.'

'But she hasn't taken refuge with you,' said Jean-Pierre.

'No, but she has left you,' said Hertz. 'I hoped you would know where she has gone.'

'Why not try Nuremberg, as you suggested? Her birth-place?'

'I will try. I feel sure she thinks of me.'

'I don't.'

Hildegard was not thinking of Dr Hertz. She hadn't given him a thought since her flight from Paris.

What she thought of now was her project of pursuing Lucan rather than being pursued. From her successful infil-tration into Maria Twickenham's house Hildegard was alive to the possibilities of combining with Lacey and Joe Murray in their search.

Hildegard was to move into Maria's flat the following Monday. She had paid a deposit. None the less, she had now no intention of occupying the flat. She meant to return to Paris and as soon as possible make Lacey and Joe serve her turn. 'Maria,' she said on the phone. 'This is Hildegard Wolf. Maria, I've been called back to Paris.'

'Oh no! That means you won't be moving in here.'

'Unfortunately no. I –'

'Your deposit . . .'

'The deposit – don't think of it.'

Maria, who needed money these days, was quite happy not to think of it. But she said, 'I'm terribly disappointed,' and meant it. She had felt the force of Hildegard's company.

'Oh, I'll be back. Let's keep in touch. You know, Maria, I think I can help Lacey with her book. I have friends who might be able to help her trace Lucan. I know he's been heard of recently around Paris. If you could give me Lacey's address or phone number in Paris I'll get in touch with her. And with Dr Murray.'

'Do you know what? I heard only last night from Lacey. They've been having a wonderful time, but they keep missing Lucan. They thought they saw him the last day of the season at Longchamp, but they were too late. It would be so thrilling for Lacey if she could locate him. Really, Hildegard, she doesn't want – neither of them wants to turn him in. She just wants an interview, anonymously, the story of his wanderings over the past twenty-five years. You need not have any fears about their turning over Lucky Lucan to the police.'

Hildegard, well insulated from such fears, took down the name and phone number of the hotel in Paris where Joe and Lacey were staying.

'Tell her,' said Maria, 'to remember that we didn't know Lucan all that closely. He played blackjack, craps, mini-bac. We played bridge.'

'I'll keep in touch with you, Maria.'

'Oh, Hildegard, yes, please do.'

Lucan had paid his cheque into the bank under the name of Walker, and had cashed a large part of it. He lost all of that at the races next day; it was a day further beclouded by rain, and disturbed by the clear, sudden sight of his two pursuers, Joe Murray and the Twickenham daughter. He thought she caught his eye, that she was very startled. He didn't wait to see how else she looked, but cleared off among the crowds which were dispersing in search of their cars or the shelter of a bar.

He was wary all the time, now, far more than in the past when he had been able to conceal his existence in one or another of Africa's vast, lesser-known territories. There, his aiders and abetters, the politicians, the heads of tribes, were sick, dead, changed or changing. Democracy was rearing its threatening head in nearly all the comfortable corners of that land. Even the simple trick of alternating his identity with that of Walker could now more easily fall foul of the law. DNA profiles and other new scientific perforations of bland surfaces were the enemy now.

Lucan, in the crumby room off the Place Vendôme which he had moved into on his return to Paris, rang the number of his former flat.

'Who's there?' It was Walker's voice. Lucky put down the phone. Walker would have to go. There was no place left for him in life's arrangements, no money to go round.

Gamblers always lose eventually, and if they can't afford to lose it is symptomatic of the situation that the wife should increasingly be blamed for the gambler's 'bad luck', and that she, in turn, should ever more display her dissatisfaction with her reduced domestic life. No household could stand firm in such circumstances. Lucan's children were not the issue; Lucan had come to detest the symbol of his bad luck: his wife and her substantial legal dues awarded by the courts, and had determined to eliminate her. He bungled.

Now Walker was taking her place. Once more, Lucan had come to the end of a cycle of fortune. Old friendships were falling off; people were dead or dying, or they were always somewhere else doing something else. Lucan was still alive? Who cared? Walker was now a liability.

Lucan remembered vividly the horror of his botched murderous attacks. In his frantic telephone calls on that night in 1974 he had reportedly muttered incoherent phrases among which the words 'mess' and 'blood' were distinguished. He now decreed to himself that there should be no blood, no mess, in the disposal of Walker.

In the meantime, having lost heavily at Longchamp, he thought he might as well call on Jean-Pierre Roget, lover of Hildegard Wolf the ex-stigmatic of Munich, to see if there was any news of her, and maybe something to collect in exchange for his dangerous knowledge.

Jean-Pierre was completing a new intricate inlay job on a chest of drawers for a museum of antique furniture, when the door of his workshop opened and in walked a good-looking, dark-haired woman of about thirty-five who seemed obviously, to Jean-Pierre's sharp mind, one of Hildegard's patients. He was right.

'I'm Mrs Maisie Round, and I've come to dialogue with you,' she declared.

'Oh, I thought you said you were going to sue for damages, Mrs Round. Has your lawyer advised against?'

'My guru suggests eyeball to eyeball, M. Roget. She's usually right.'

'You know,' said Jean-Pierre, 'I'm not in touch with Hildegard.'

'I have to dialogue. I have come to this venue to address the problem that Dr Wolf has left me traumatically in mid-air. At the end of the day, instead of being cured I'm a worse wreck than before. I missed out on a marriage proposal. I want to stipulate that if this situation perpetuates I will need to have recourse to help in a private assisted-living facility.'

'Can't your guru assist you in this –'

A tall man had entered the shop. That melon-shaped head . . . Walker? – No, Lucky Lucan. He had entered before he could see Maisie Round standing behind Jean-Pierre at his workbench.

'Lord Lucan,' said Jean-Pierre, 'may I present Mrs Maisie Round, another of Dr Wolf's patients?'

'Lord Lucan!' she said.

'Lord Lucan had turned and walked swiftly out of the

workshop. He could be seen hailing a taxi at the end of the street.

'He'll be back,' said Jean-Pierre. 'He's looking for money.'

'Am I crazy or is that the Lucan who murdered the nanny years ago?'

'You are right on both counts. Now I have to close shop, I'm afraid. I am late for a lunch date, hence the confusion.'

Walker was crossing Paris in a taxi. He had seemed to spend a great deal of his life crossing cities in taxis. Lima, Rio, Boston, Glasgow, London, not to speak of Bulawayo, Lagos, Nairobi. All to get from one point to another in aid of Lucan. Now it was Paris, north-east to south, from a Banque Suisse to a Credit Lyonnais and this time with no hope whatsoever in his heart. The account in the first bank had been closed, all the assets withdrawn in two operations, one day following the other, and this was, again, a day after a large deposit had been made in the name of Walker. Lucan must have returned to Paris, he must have gone to some gambling place (or, let's think, yes, the last week of Longchamp) and cleaned out the Scottish connection loot. Now, if there was nothing deposited in the Lyonnais, Walker was practically penniless, alone in a rented apartment, the rent of which had been owing for eight weeks. Shortly, he would be homeless.

And shortly, having discovered that his account in the French bank was also empty, he was on his way, in the Metro, to Jean-Pierre's workshop.

'No,' said Jean-Pierre, when Walker made directly plain his need for 'a loan'. 'Walker,' said Jean-Pierre, 'you are Lucan, in which case you are wanted for murder and attempted murder, or you are Lucan's double, guilty of the offence of aiding and abetting a criminal in his long-term evasion of the law; in other words you are a couple of criminals and you can kindly step out of my workshop.'

'The story of Beate Pappenheim is not very pretty. The old warrant for her arrest has not been lifted.'

'Don't waste my time. It works both ways.'

'We are more elusive than Hildegard.'

A man came in, and got Jean-Pierre's immediate attention. Walker said, 'I'll be back later,' and left. The man was looking for an antique fire-guard, two of which Jean-Pierre was able to produce. There was a good deal of discussion and measuring. Finally the customer chose one, paid, and carried it away under his arm. As he left the shop another man stood in the doorway. The new arrival now entered. He was the African, Dr Jacobs.

'Do you have news?' said Dr Jacobs.

'I do. I've tracked her down to a hotel in London, where she's booked in under her own name, Dr Wolf. She doesn't know it, but I'm leaving tonight for London, where I'll join her.'

'Tell her I've been anxious. I want to resume our sessions.'

'If you really want Hildegard back, you can help me to rid her of a couple of nuisances. Two old men. They are making her life a hell, and she's on the run from them, only from them.'

'How can I help?'

'Africa,' said Jean-Pierre. 'They have been in Africa before, and to Africa they should return.' Jean-Pierre had poured wine for them both and he now pulled round a second chair from the other side of his workbench. They sat talking for two hours, at the end of which Jean-Pierre said, 'Karl Jacobs, you are a true friend.'

'Yes, I think so, Jean-Pierre Roget. I think, always, that I have that talent, to be a true friend.'

When Jean-Pierre entered the lobby of the hotel at Queen's Gate where Hildegard was staying, there was only a young student-like man sitting in a chair reading the *Evening Standard*, and a blonde woman in a black-and-white suit at the desk. By the door were some small pieces of luggage. It was nearly nine-thirty. Jean-Pierre went over to the desk to ask for Hildegard. The woman had paid her bill and now folded it away in her bag. She started towards the door.

'Hildegard!' He was so astonished to see her with her newly fair head of hair that he didn't know quite what to say. He said, 'Will you marry me?'

'What should I do that for?' she said, not knowing, either, exactly what to say.

'Your convalescent widower, Hertz, wants to marry you.'

'I'll have to consult my assistant, Dominique. She's been married twice. What brings you here?'

'You,' he said.

'Well, we're going right back. I'm the pursuer now, and I have the address of a couple of people who are on Lucan's trail in Paris. They've seen him, he keeps evading them but they've seen him.'

17

Tall Walker, having obtained a temporary job as a Père Nöel in a Paris department store, could count on a modest pay for a few weeks ahead. He rather liked the job and fancied he suited it well.

But Walker was weary. The furnished flat comprised two rooms, a kitchen and a bathroom. Lucky normally occupied the bedroom, while Walker slept on a divan in the sitting-room. The place had been decorated by someone with a mania for stripes, pale stripes on the wallpaper, louder ones on the upholstery throughout the apartment. The bathroom tiles formed red stripes punctuated by little bunches of cherries and rosebuds. The towels were striped. The stripes in the sitting-room were green and white. The wall-to-wall stuff on the floor, discernible as a yellowish green by origin, was now a matted and stained old brown. A tap in the bathroom dripped incessantly but Walker didn't feel like approaching the concierge about it; there was the question of the overdue rent which the husband of the concierge ferociously wanted.

Now Walker was idly practising his part before a mirror above the mantelpiece; it seemed to him that he had been attitudinising most of his life. He had been the perfect English butler in Mexico, he had been Lucky Lucan for over ten years in Central Africa, and recently in Paris; and now Father Christmas at the Bon Marché.

A key in the lock of the front door. Lucky Lucan walked in, not a hair out of place. He held a white carrier bag from which he extracted a bottle of whisky. He put it down on a side table with a thud.

'Where have you been?'

Lucan, on his return from the kitchen with two glasses and a bowl of ice, said, 'Where have I been and what have I done with the money? I might just as well have stayed with my wife. Well, I've had a run of bad luck.'

'I know we're absolutely broke.'

'No,' said Lucan, 'I've just come back from Roget's junk shop. I didn't expect him to let me in, but do you know, he did willingly. I had a long talk with him. We're in business again, we have to go back to Africa.'

'Oh, God! Impossible!'

'Can't be helped. It's inevitable. It's a question of one of these tribal chiefs wanting an English tutor for his children. Two English tutors would be even more accept-able. The utmost discretion about us. His grandson is a Dr Karl Jacobs – here's his card – lives in Paris. There are three sons. No further questions asked. He wants them to grow up like English lords. That's where I fit the bill.'

'Do you trust Jacobs?'

'I shouldn't think so. I haven't met him. But we've noth-ing much to lose. We've no option, in fact.'

'And Roget?'

'I don't trust him. He's a swine, besides. He makes it a condition that we take this job in Africa. A condition. Otherwise he'll expose us.'

'But Hildegard . . .'

'He tells me Hildegard is well protected. She has the means to defend herself, we don't. And that's maybe the truth. Roget tried to follow me here in a taxi. Some hope! He failed.'

'How much did you get in Scotland?'

'Mind your own business.'

'Haven't you any other old friends?'

'Plenty. One of them has a daughter who wants to get at me. She wants an interview. Writing a book. She's going around with an old gambling friend of mine, Joe Murray. Her mother was Maria Twickenham. They even got on the same plane to Paris as I did. It was touch and go. They half recognised me and half didn't, and then it was too late, you know how it is.'

'I can get a job as a butler again, any time, Lucky. You can count me out of Africa.'

'Oh no I can't. I can make trouble for you and you know it.'

'Not so much as I could make for you.'

'Try it, then.'

It occurred to Walker that much the same conversation had been repeated between them for years; for years on end. He would go to Africa because Lucky Lucan said so.

'I hope,' he said, 'that it will be a comfortable job.'

'Very comfortable. Every comfort,' said Lucan.

'What part exactly?'

'It's a small independent tribal state, north of the Congo, called Kanzia.'

'I've heard of it. A small diamond mine, but extra-large diamonds,' said Walker.

'That's it. And some copper. They do well. They import most things, including equipment for their very decent-sized army.'

'Too hot,' said Walker.

'The Chief's residence has air-conditioning.'

'The Chief?'

'His name's Kanzia, like the place. He calls himself the Paramount Chief. He has a jacuzzi bath,' Lucan said.

'I could swear,' said Lacey, 'that I even saw him dressed as Santa Claus in a department store. Something about his shape, and very tall, no kidding.'

This gave rise to another explosion of laughter all round. There were Lacey, Joe, Jean-Pierre, Hildegard, Dominique, Paul and Dick, with the help of Olivia, all dining together in Hildegard's flat. It was a remarkably happy evening. Lacey, now due home for her children's holidays, had decided to give up her quest. She was recounting with much merriment the number of occasions on which they had missed Lucan by a hair's breadth, and the other occasions on which Joe was either too late or completely mistaken.

'We did really see him on the plane. At Longchamp almost surely. But then Joe had a sighting at a lecture at the British Council. Now, if there is one place Lucan would not be, it would be a lecture at the British Council. A lecture on Ford Madox Ford.'

'And then, you say he was Father Christmas . . .' said Hildegard.

'That takes the biscuit,' said Joe.

'Well, we've had a good time, Joe and I,' said Lacey. 'It's a pity we never caught up with him after all this effort.'

'He would never have let you interview him.'

'You think not? Even for old friends like Joe and my mother?'

'I don't know,' said Hildegard. They had not been told about Lucan's double. It would be too much for them to take in with all these breaths of happiness they were experiencing. Even a simple manhunt had been so peripheral to their love affair that they had let him slip time and again, and enjoyed it.

'I daresay he'll go back to Africa,' said Jean-Pierre. 'That's where he always feels most secure, I imagine.'

'Oh, surely,' said Hildegard.

'I'm looking forward to getting back to normal, actually,' said Lacey.

'Me, too,' said Hildegard. 'I'm opening my office again next week.'

18

Kanzia was a thickly forested territory of about thirty square kilometres, within which was a clearing on a rocky plateau of about five square kilometres. It was bounded by a wide, reedy swamp in the north, a tributary river in the east, a lake in the south and an enemy in the west. That hostile neighbour kept the considerable armed forces of Kanzia constantly on the alert, and was generally useful when the Chief, old Delihu Kanzia, wanted to pick a fight to divert his people's cravings for such indigestible ideas as democracy. As the Chief's grandson, Karl Jacobs, had told Jean-Pierre, the tiny state was renowned for its having extracted over the years an exceptional number of extra-large diamond lumps, from a mine that as yet showed no signs of petering out.

The Chief was supremely happy when his grandson, Karl, in Paris, sent him word by fax that a couple of English earls had been engaged to tutor his three sons, aged thirteen, fifteen and eighteen. He had other small children, but they could benefit from the prestigious village school of Kanzia in the meantime.

For the last lap of their journey Lucky and Walker were borne each on a slung couch attached to four poles. They had left the jeep at the edge of the forest; the rest of the way was a footpath.

'Flies, flies again,' said Lucan. 'People who don't know Africa don't know how thick with flies the air is everywhere. Nobody writes about the flies. Flies, mosquitoes, flying ants, there's no end to them.' He flourished a fly swat that one of his bearers had handed to him. They passed a woman with a child on her back, its eyes and mouth black with crawling flies. In Africa there was nothing to be done, ever, about the flies.

Lucan's four men sweated under their burden. They talked loudly all the way, shouting back also to Walker's bearers.

The Chief was impatient for their arrival. 'What are two English earls doing here in these parts? They have committed crimes?' the wily fellow had asked one of his henchmen.

'Well, one of them is a nanny-basher.'

'What is a nanny?'

'I think it's some kind of an enemy.'

'Then he's a brave man, no?'

'These are Christians. They might bring us a holy scripture and a string of beads. Take no notice.'

'Oh Christians worship the Lamb, unlike the Hindus who worship the Cow. They wash in the blood of a lamb.'

'I don't know about that. I should think it was a sticky way to be washed.'

'They say it makes them white, the blood of the lamb.'

'They're inscrutable, these people, but Karl says they are noblemen.'

Delihu had sent his strongest bearers with their litters and arranged for a long strip of red carpet to be spread down the front steps of his large dwelling.

19

Hildegard's business flourished over the following months. She disposed of most of the patients she had left behind when she went to London, for she did not believe in long-term therapy. New patients abounded; she seemed to have the healing touch. She now also returned to her domestic life with Jean-Pierre, untroubled and unmarried as always.

One day in the cold early spring of the following year, Dominique rang through to Hildegard while she was with a patient; this was an unusual procedure.

'Dr Karl Jacobs is here to see you personally.'

'Good. Tell him to wait.'

When his turn came round she greeted him warmly. 'We're in your debt, Dr Jacobs. It's wonderful in Paris these days without the Lucan menace. I hope . . .'

'I bring you information.'

'About them?'

Karl Jacobs began his story:

'You know, my grandfather believed they were both English earls. No matter, let him believe. The three sons did very well under their tuition. They learnt to jump their horses over fences, they learnt to cheat at poker and so on, in the best tradition of a gentleman. The only difficulty was between the two lords. Lord Lucan was hearing voices, and Lord Walker was also assailed by unaccountable fears which I can assure you are peculiar to white people in central Africa.

'My grandfather Delihu was convinced Walker was bewitched, which is always possible in that land. Walker complained that the sun went down too quickly and the long starry nights chilled his soul. Lucan wanted to poison Walker; his voices recommended it. But Chief Delihu Kanzia objected. If you poison a man, you see, Dr Wolf, you can't eat him. My grandfather thought it over, and was advised by the good people of our medicinal miracles that the boys would benefit by consuming an earl; they would become, in effect, Earl Walkers if they should eat Walker. Which is logical – no?'

'Yes,' said Hildegard. 'That's very logical. We become in some measure what we eat, not to mention what we see, hear and smell. The only difficulty is, as you know, Walker is not an earl. Lucan is the earl.'

'No matter,' said Jacobs, 'there was a mistake. Two strong men were set to wait for Walker one night when he was returning from his walk to the Palace Paramount where he had a fine apartment for himself – my grandfather was very benevolent towards him. The men clubbed him to death, only it wasn't Walker, it was Lucan. Such a quantity of blood, my grandfather said . . . The lords were practically identical, except that Lucan was a better teacher. Walker did not have much to teach except fear of the stars.'

'Lucan is dead and buried, then?'

'Lucan is dead, not buried. He was roasted and consumed by all the male children of Delihu. Some of them were rather unwell after the feast, but they are all partly little Lord Lucans now.'

'And Walker?'

'My grandfather discerned that Walker had been spared by unseen spirits of destiny. He has gone to Mexico. My kind grandfather paid his fare. I travelled to Kanzia myself

131

to escort him to an airport. The tribespeople did not care for him at all. They preferred Lucan. But Walker got away. I even helped him to pack his few poor things, and I gave him some of my grandfather's dollars to help him out.'

'It's good of you to come and tell me this, Dr Jacobs.'

'Oh, but I like you so much, Dr Wolf. You've given me such courage to work here in Paris. What I especially came for was to bring you a message that Walker gave me with instructions to send it by e-mail to the German and French consuls in Chad.'

He handed over to Hildegard a handwritten sheet of blue Basildon Bond writing paper. On it was written:

Pappenheim Beate, fraudulent stigmatic of Munich, year 1978 forward, is now a successful psychiatrist in Paris under the false name of Dr Hildegard Wolf. Her sumptuous offices are in the Boulevard St Germain.

'You promised to send this?' said Hildegard.

'Of course. But again, of course, I didn't. In any case the consuls would have thought it mad.'

Hildegard said, 'I appreciate your kindness,' but she obviously meant much more.

'Tear it up,' said Karl K. Jacobs.

She did just that. She looked round the office. It looked cleaner than usual.